THE PRINCESS BELLAHELD

TIMELESS CHRISTIAN CLASSICS
from GENERATIONS

Heidi

The Holy War

The Pilgrim's Progress for Young Readers

Robinson Crusoe

The Swiss Family Robinson

Titus: A Comrade of the Cross

The Life of Henry Martyn

The Dragon and the Raven

Sunshine Country

The Princess Bellaheld

The Giant Killer

Mary Jones and Her Bible

THE PRINCESS BELLAHELD

Julie Sutter
Edited by Perry and Kimberly Coghlan

Generations
PASSING ON THE FAITH

Copyright © 2021 by Generations

All rights reserved.
Printed in Korea.

ISBN: 978-1-954745-06-3

Interior Layout Design: Zane McMinn, Joshua Schwisow
Cover Design: Justin Turley
Cover Artwork: iStock.com

Originally published as *Bilihild: A Tale of the Irish Missionaries in Germany, A.D. 703* by Julie Sutter, The Religious Tract Society, London, 1899.

Generations
19039 Plaza Dr. Ste. 210
Parker, Colorado 80134
www.generations.org

For more information on this and other titles from Generations, visit *www.generations.org* or call *888-389-9080*.

Contents

Preface 6
Original Preface and Historical Note 8
Germany A.D. 700 10
Cast of Characters 11
Chapter 1: A Dying Mother 13
Chapter 2: Gisilhar of the Arch 27
Chapter 3: A Noble Suitor 45
Chapter 4: Mother and Wife 61
Chapter 5: The Wild Hunt 75
Chapter 6: Ill Weeds Grow Apace 85
Chapter 7: Patient in Tribulation 105
Chapter 8: Trouble and Escape 115
Chapter 9: Peace at Last 125
Glossary of Terms 141
The Irish Communion Hymn 145

PREFACE

We live in a day that has stolen our sense of history. We live in a time that has forgotten God's providential plan and how He works all things together for good. I am a father on a mission to recapture the memory of the wonderful works the Lord has done so that my children understand how God cares for us, His people. My wife Kim and I are always on the lookout for books that will help us in this task.

You can imagine her delight when, at a recent book sale, among the old magazines and other ancient ephemera she spotted a dusty little hardback subtitled "A Tale of the Irish Missionaries in Germany 703." For the last year we had been studying church history as a family and had begun to have a sense of the string of small stories scattered through history like pearls. Small and precious, their value lies not in their uniqueness but in their similarity. They are the tales of providence and care, left as clues by our spiritual forefathers to give us hope. This little book is one of those pearls.

Yet we were doubly surprised and thrilled to find that our little book held not just a tale of missionaries, but that of a young heroine. We had discovered the account of a brave young girl—originally named Bilihild—who endured harsh persecution but rested in God's promises; who faced a strong temptation to fall, yet stood fast by strength greater than her own. My wife, herself the oldest of ten girls, has remarked on the apparent dearth of strong, godly young heroines in either fact or fiction. This is one of the many reasons our family came to love this story. Here we found an example of feminine boldness, courage and faith. The life of Bilihild exemplified a type of strength that has nothing to do with feminism and everything to do with true Biblical femininity.

So I hope you find, as we did, encouragement from the example of a girl from the past as you seek to inspire the mothers of the future.

While reading, keep an eye out for numbers marked on special terms. Those numbers are keyed to the glossary in the back of the book. The glossary provides brief definitions for unfamiliar terms.

Perry and Kimberly Coghlan

ORIGINAL PREFACE AND HISTORICAL NOTE

This little tale, retold rather than translated, is taken from the German of Professor Ebrard of Erlangen, to whom we are indebted for much information concerning the early Church of Ireland and Scotland, known in ecclesiastical history as the Culdean Church.

This story (of a young girl originally known as Bilihild) carries us back more than a thousand years, to the first growth of Christianity, which now spreads as a mighty tree. In that time the Church of Ireland shone as a very star in the West. Her learned men were the pride of courts, and her missionaries carried the pure Gospel far and wide. Germany and Switzerland to a great extent were Christianized from Ireland.

The early Church of Ireland was eminently a mission Church; and the manner in which she set to work was not without a tinge of colonization. Her messengers went forth by bands of twelves: twelve brethren under an abbot (a church leader or elder), with their wives and families—forming the nucleus, as it were, of a community—would found their cenoby in the wilds of some heathen land, bringing their influence to bear upon the people round about them—their charity, that is, winning them to the Lord; the cenoby growing and sending forth new bands of workers to found new settlements elsewhere.

It was the Culdean Church, and not Rome, which in this manner was chiefly instrumental in Christianizing the heart of Western Europe.

For derivation of the "Culdee," setting aside others, we give Professor Ebrard's definition, from the Gaelic *cele* (fellow, or man) and *De* (God): at any rate, "men of God" the Irish missionaries were called by the heathen wherever they went.

Bilihild (known as the Princess Bellaheld in this publication) and Hedan are no fiction; the "men of God" occurring in these pages one and all are historic; and the little story, in the best and deepest sense, is true.

Julie Sutter

GERMANY
A.D. 700

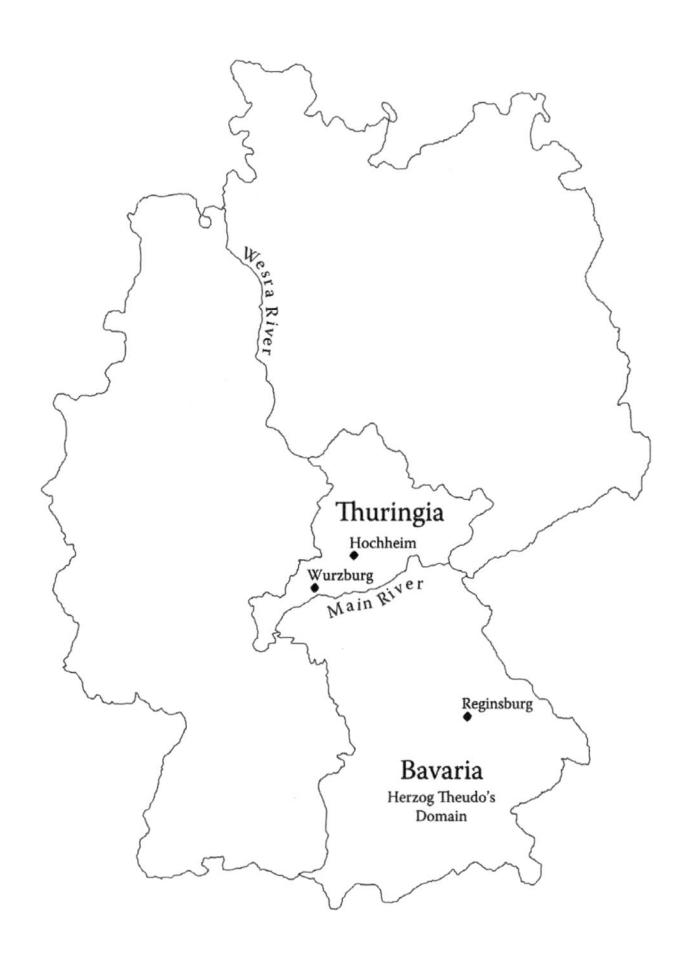

Wesra River

Thuringia

Hochheim

Wurzburg

Main River

Reginsburg

Bavaria

Herzog Theudo's
Domain

CAST OF CHARACTERS

Bellaheld
The young daughter of missionaries from Ireland who also has the title of Herzogin

Totman
A close friend of Bellaheld's late father

Abbot Colman
Abbot of the cenoby at Hocheim

Abbot David
Abbot of the cenoby at Wirtsburg

Gozbert
The Christian Herzog (or Duke) of Thuringia

Hedan
The son of the Gozbert, next in line to rule Thuringia; also goes by the title of Herzog

Geila
The heathen wife of Herzog (or Duchess) Gozbert, and Hedan's mother

Pillung
A heathen manservant in the house of the Herzog

Hezzilo
A pagan high priest

Regiswind
Geila's waiting woman

Haimerich
A Christian retainer in the service of the Herzog

Gisilhar
A free lord in the service of Herzog Theudo

Mechild
The mother of Bellaheld and the wife of Iberius, who was a missionary from Ireland

CHAPTER 1

A DYING MOTHER

I am a stranger with Thee, and a sojourner, as all my fathers were.
—Psalm 39:12

In a small low-thatched cabin, roughly built of wood, lay a woman past middle life, with sunken eyes and the flush of fever on her cheeks. Her couch was a broad wooden bench, her covering a couple of bearskins. Her clothing consisted of an ample garment of undyed sheep's wool. Beside the bed, if such it could be called, an earthenware jug, filled with spring water, was placed on a log within the reach of her feeble hands. A younger woman, similarly dressed, sat at a little distance. The cabin stood within a hundred yards of the German river Main, but the two women spoke not the German tongue.

"I have longed for this day," said the sick woman, "with the longing of the swallow for the southern land, when the leaves are gathering their autumn tints. On some sea-girt rock the weary bird might be resting, lonely and sad; the waving palm-trees would beckon her onward to that other shore, but the wing is powerless to reach it. See, the day has come, the blessed Easter day! Protected by the God-fearing Herzog[1], the Christian flock will unite at the oratory[2] beneath the Wirtsburg[3] to witness with praise and thanksgiving the baptism of my beloved daughter, my only child. The river flowing past our cenoby[4] has touched there, each wave seems burdened with a message to me: 'The festal time is at hand,' I hear them saying. The bells proclaim it from the tower, 'Come! Come!' they say, 'and tarry not.' But Bellaheld's mother is lying low in sickness. I feel the shadows of death closing about me."

"Let not thy heart be troubled, sister Mechild," replied her companion, "but yield it to the will of God. His thoughts are thoughts of peace, and not of evil. In the body thou art absent from thy daughter's baptism, but thy prayers for her may rise to God, bringing thee very near to her, even in Him."

"Thou art right," said the sick woman, "and death with Him is powerless. 'Christ is the resurrection and the life: he that believeth in Him, though he were dead, yet shall live.' Iberius, my husband, also lives, though with mortal eyes I saw his face grow white in death. He too, in the spirit, will be with his child; her father's blessing will descend on her."

She ceased speaking, folding her hands in silence, then she continued, "My child will be baptized this day, but I enter the gates of death. The sun has risen brightly. Before it setteth I shall be gone. See, the morn is breaking which knoweth no going down. The weary feet are coming home—ah, weary indeed! How long it is since they began their earthly course in the green isle—how far away! At Armagh, in distant Erin[5], Aghandekka was born—yes, Mechild would have liked to see the place again where she was called Aghandekka—her childhood's home."

"These all died in faith," responded the younger woman, in the words of the Apostle, "not having received the promises, but having seen them afar off, and were persuaded of them, and embraced them, and confessed that they were strangers and pilgrims on the earth. For they that say such things declare plainly that they seek a country. And truly, if they had been mindful of that country from whence they came out, they might have had opportunity to have returned. But now they desire a better country, that is, an heavenly: where God is not ashamed to be called their God, for He hath prepared for them a city."

"Hark!" said Mechild, "I hear the bell calling to prayer. Leave me, dearest Gertrude. Go, join our brothers and sisters in the oratory."

"Leave thee? No," replied the latter, "comforting the sick is no less a service to Him than joining with the congregation; and where two or three are gathered in His name, He is in the midst of them. Thou and I may worship Him here. What wouldst thou have me read?"

"Thou art kind, Gertrude. The Lord will be thy reward. I would hear the Savior's parting words to His disciples, as given in the Gospel of St. John."

Gertrude, rising from her seat, took a parchment roll from a shelf beneath the thatch. It contained the four Gospels in the Irish language, carefully written and partly illuminated. She was just about to begin her reading, when the door opened and a venerable figure entered, saying, "Peace be with you." The old man's hair was silvery white, but it was allowed to grow at the back only, the front to the crown of his head being closely shaven. His dress consisted of a simple tunic of undyed wool, and leathern shoes with leggings reaching to the knees. In his right hand he held a chalice, his left bearing the bread. A pouch was suspended from his belt.

"Is it thou, Totman!" exclaimed the sick woman, her face flushing eagerly. "Comest thou to me, thou friend of my departed husband, rather than join in the service?"

"Yes, sister Aghandekka," answered the aged man with a smile. "Abbot Colman has sent me; the stricken widow of a faithful messenger of Christ shall not be left to hunger while the congregation has meat and drink in the house of God. I have come to read the Scriptures with thee, and we three will remember the Lord's death as He would have us. It is the worthy Abbot who thus thought of thy spiritual need, and his wife has not left thy body to want. A bottle of milk I have for thee, and a barley cake, which she gave me, that thou mayest eat and drink when we have worshipped the Lord."

And he took from the pouch by his side a silver flask containing wine, then a stone bottle filled with milk, and the cake in question. The earthly food was placed on the floor, while the wooden log beside the bed served as a table during the Communion about to be celebrated.

The aged priest, or presbyter, knelt by the sick woman, and having chanted, "Glory be to the Father, and to the Son, and to the Holy Ghost," he repeated the Lord's Prayer, to which he added a few words of loving intercession for the maiden who, at that self-same hour, was to be received into the Church. Having recommended the dying mother to the Lord of mercy, he then took up the Gospel and read the very words she had longed for; those words of tender comfort which Christ gave to His disciples.

He added no sermon to the lesson, but addressed the weary pilgrim with kindly words of sympathy; their experience had been a common one for many a year.

"Let me look back with thee to the time," he began, "when, following Killean, the blessed man of God who has since gone to glory, our little band left the green shores of Ireland to bring the Gospel to the poor heathen on this great continent. 'In the world ye shall have tribulation,' said the venerable Abbot-Bishop Columba, as we set sail on our mission, but he could add the Lord's words, 'Be of good cheer, I have overcome the world.' How truly have we found it so! Our very voyage was troubled and stormy, deep calling unto deep. Our women and little ones, nay ourselves, looked despondingly into the watery gulf. Killean alone kept his faith, believing even as St. Paul believed on the terrible sea. And we were brought safe to land, casting anchor on the shores of Friesland.

"We sailed up the Rhine as far as the Roman colony, Moguntia[6], where the great German river receives the darker waters of the Main. There we found a Christian settlement ruled over by Bishop Buaidhe, or Sigfrid, as they call him here, thine own brother. Of him we inquired whither we should direct our steps, anxious as we were to work for the Lord. He advised us to turn our ship's head up the Main to the land of the Thuringians, a fine people, lost in the night of paganism. They were ruled over by their Herzog, Gozbert, who, although a heathen, was a brave and noble hero. It is just eighteen years ago; it was in the year of our Lord 685 that we arrived at the foot of the Wirtsburg. The Herzog received us hospitably and inquired about our plans. We acknowledged ourselves messengers of the Lord God, the Maker of heaven and earth. We told him we were sent to tell him of a new kingdom of peace and righteousness established by One in whose Name the Gentiles also shall trust, and behold, he was anxious to be taught. He gave us leave to settle at the foot of his Wirtsburg, between the hillside and the river. There we erected an oratory, our place of worship, built of stone, and around it thirteen wooden cabins, one for the Abbot and his wife, and one for each of the brethren with their families, also a common refectory[7] and barns. The settlement was enclosed with a ring-fence. The river yielded plenty of fish for food, and we planted a few vines on the hill side, having brought them from Moguntia, that we might celebrate the Holy Communion. And thus we began to preach Christ crucified, finding open ears and willing hearts among the Thuringians.

"The Herzog himself heard us often and gladly, but he would not decide for baptism because his wife, the Herzogin Geila, strove hard for the heathen practices. For the priests of their false gods, Woden and Friga, Thor and Eor, perceiving the people were inclined to Christianity, had threatened the Herzogin with dire consequences, and she worked upon the Herzog her husband. It so happened that a horde of Chawari, a wild Asiatic people which had followed the course of the Danube, just about this time broke into the land and burnt the villages of the unwary Thuringians. Geila said it was Woden's revenge, because his worship had been neglected, and that the enemy could not be driven back unless Herzog Gozbert would appease the injured gods by sacrificing the blaspheming foreigners on the forsaken altars.

"Gozbert listened to her evil counsel. Father Killean and our brethren Galun and Arnuval were seized and killed by the bloodthirsty priests. We others fled like frightened sheep, and for a time lived in the forest, building huts here at Hochheim, and not venturing back to the Wirtsburg. But the Herzog gathered the strength of his land about him, and the Chawari, finding themselves outnumbered, withdrew beyond the frontier. Then he imagined it was the gods who had helped him because of his yielding up the Christian messengers.

"Yet see, before the year had waned, the Chawari had returned in tenfold number, burning and murdering with ruthless fury. The word, 'In the world ye shall have tribulation,' was now doubly true with us, for we were in twofold anguish, terror of the Chawari on the one hand and fear of the Herzog on the other, being all the time as men on a burning vessel, fire behind us and water beyond. The people from everywhere fled to the Wirtsburg, to the strong enclosure. But how could we go there for shelter, being in bodily fear of the Herzog himself?

"In that time of distress, when the hosts of the Chawari were within half a day's march of us on the other side of the river, it was Iberius, thy husband, who raised his voice in counsel, saying, 'If death be our meet, brethren, let us rather die as confessors witnessing for the Lord, than be killed by the Chawari away from our post. Up! Then, to the Wirtsburg! Let us ask the weak-hearted ruler, Is this the help thou hast experienced at the hands of thy gods? Trust thou in the living God, and He alone will save thee.'

"Thus spoke Iberius the faithful, and we obeyed his voice.

Together with many other fugitives, we arrived at the Wirtsburg. Bellaheld, thy child, was then a babe only ten weeks old. But one of Geila's men-at-arms, seeing us return, threw a stone towards us as we entered the enclosure; it hit Iberius, crushing his shoulder. He lingered a few weeks and died, leaving thee a widow and thy babe fatherless. Thus the word came home to thee also, 'In the world ye shall have tribulation.'

"But thy husband did not die without tasting fullness of the promise, 'Be of good cheer, I have overcome the world.' It was our Abbot who went up to the Herzog, bravely asking the question, 'What is it thy gods have done for thee, or the blood of the saints thou hast spilt?'

"And Gozbert trembled. 'Show me that He whom thou worshippest is mightier than the gods of my fathers and I will believe,' said he.

"But Colman made answer, 'That thy fathers' gods have availed thee nothing, thou hast seen with thine eyes. The living God who made heaven and earth alone can help thee. He can confound thine enemies, and let them be as chaff before the wind. He can do it, if it pleaseth Him; but only if thou wilt repent thee of thy great sin and come to Him for mercy.'

" 'I will, but pray thou for me,' said Gozbert, humbled. 'I am altogether undone, my men are destroyed, I have but women and children left within the ring-fence. Pray for me!'

" 'I will,' replied Colman; 'but thou must join us thyself, lifting up thy voice to the Lord of mercy.'

"Night was falling when Father Colman spoke thus. The Herzog placed watchmen upon the turrets and returned with us to the foot of the mount where our settlement had been. The cabins were burnt to the ground, but the oratory, the strong stone tower, remained standing. We entered, the

Herzog along with us. And now Colman began chanting the penitential psalms in the German language that Gozbert might understand. Lowly upon his knees he chanted verse after verse. And kneeling around him in deep contrition we repeated after him, Gozbert with us, verse upon verse. Thus we continued far into the night, the lamp shedding a subdued radiance about us.

"At midnight the watchmen on the tower heard a clattering noise in the valley, as of a host of warriors nearing from the direction of the burnt-down cabins. They listened, fearful of what might befall their Herzog. When the approaching host had seemingly reached the stone tower, the clanking suddenly ceased, as though they were pausing. Presently the watchmen on the Wirtsburg heard a strange rustling from the valley, as of a swarm of cranes rising on their wings, or a herd of deer breaking through the brushwood. It died away in the distance, and all was still. When the morning rose, they descended from the Burg to look for the Herzog, and behold! The place all round was strewn with spears and battleaxes, left behind by the Chawari in their headlong flight. They had chosen that very night for an attack, and coming forth from the forest, they had suddenly seen the soft gleaming light of the lamp burning within the oratory. They had heard the low chanting, and a terror from the Lord had fallen upon them. They had fled, truly, as chaff before the wind, and no mortal eye in the this neighborhood has seen them since.

"Then Herzog Gozbert believed, and was baptized, having been instructed in the truth, as is meet. The cenoby at the foot of the Wirtsburg was built up again, and more brethren arrived with Abbot David, to the sore grief of the Herzogin Geila. We others, with our own Abbot Colman, returned hither to continue at the new settlement. Thou also didst come back with us to Hochheim, leaving behind thee Bellaheld, thy little daughter, that she might be taught at Wirtsburg in the school which thy brother Edda with his wife had founded there.

"Thou knowest all this history which I have thus called up to thy memory, for it is thine own history, and yet I told it as though it were unknown to thee, wishing to bring back thy past life to thy inward eye, that, having reached unto the end, thou mayest look upon the road by which the Lord hath brought thee. The ways have been rough, and yet they have been ways of peace, for their end is salvation. Thou knewest it would be so, when thou followedst the presbyter and messenger, Iberius, as his wedded wife. Thou knewest that all earthly pleasure, even this life's happiness, must be laid upon the altar that souls might be won for Him from the heathen people who knew Him not, and yet are precious in His sight. For they also are bought with a price. But thou wast willing to bear thy part in the blessed work. And the first-fruits have been given us. Hundreds of those among whom we spend our life, who were born in darkness, put now their trust in the grace of God which is in Christ Jesus, and have given up all evil practices and deeds of wickedness.

"Ought we not to return thanks to Him, saying, 'We are not worthy of the least of all the mercies and of all the truth which Thou has showed unto Thy servants'? Alas! How often have we been wanting in love, in patience, in faith. How often have we even murmured at the tribulation which we must have in the world, forgetting in our faithless grief that we have every right to be of good cheer through Him who has overcome the world? Is the place which He has prepared for us not enough? And as regards this world, Aghandekka, is it not more than enough that the Lord has put thy beloved child from her earliest youth into the way of salvation? It is true that today it is not given thee to clasp her to thy heart, but art thou not satisfied that thy Savior will take her to His heart as a lamb to His bosom, while thou art near her in prayer? She will now be made a partaker of the covenant, and for the first time this day she will join the congregation in the Communion of His body and blood. And thou, too, art about to join in this. Repent thee humbly of thy sins and thy many shortcomings, remembering that the Bread of Life is given to the hungry."

Totman knelt down, engaging in a short but earnest prayer, which the sick woman repeated after him and, having broken the bread and poured the wine into the chalice, he began slowly and solemnly to sing the communion hymn of the Irish Church. Gertrude reverently joined in the singing, while the dying Mechild worshipped her Redeemer in fainting notes. The hymn they sung has been rendered into many of the modern languages of Europe. It presents in clear and lively form the faith of the early Irish Church. It is more evangelical in its teaching than might have been expected in that age, and there is ample evidence of the fact that in the eighth century the Irish branch of the Church was one of the purest in this respect. The following is a recent translation of some of the stanzas:

Salvation's given, Christ the only Son,
By His dear Cross and Blood the victory won.

Offered was He for greatest and for least,
Himself the Victim and Himself the Priest.

*He, Ransomer from death, and Light from shade,
Now gives His holy grace His saints to aid.*

*He, that in this world rules His saints and shields,
To all believers life eternal yields.*

*With heavenly bread makes them that hunger whole,
Gives living waters to the thirsting soul.*

*Alpha and Omega, to Whom shall bow
All nations at the Doom, is with us now.*

When they had sung this hymn, the aged minister gave the bread and the wine to the two women before him, after which he repeated the Nunc Dimittis[8], also the Lord's Prayer, and kneeling again, he concluded the service as he had began it, repeating, "Glory be to the Father, and to the Son and to the Holy Ghost."

"How shall I thank you for this comfort in my dying hour?" said Mechild, adding after awhile, "Tell good mother Hilda how grateful I am for her kindness in sending me this bread and milk to refresh me. But I think the bread which the Lord has just blessed to me will be the last I shall have need of in my pilgrimage. Earthly food can no longer avail me. The end is near. The eye is growing dim. Ah, my child, had I once more seen thee!"

The words had scarcely escaped her lips when the door was thrown open eagerly, and a maiden, fair as the morning, hastened to the bedside. "Mother! Mother!" she exclaimed, sinking to her knees by her dying parent.

"Bellaheld!" faltered Mechild, "is it thou? Can I indeed bless thee ere I go?" She placed her trembling hands on the girl's head, her lips moving in prayer which none but God could hear. The light fled from her face; she lay still in death.

It was a happy death, and her desire had been given her; she had seen her child before she went. When Bellaheld had spent her first grief, clasping the lifeless hand, Totman asked her gently, "How was it possible to come so quickly? It is barely time for the service to have been finished."

"Alas, reverend Father," sobbed the orphaned maiden, "the service was never begun. I am as yet unbaptized, and have fled hither for fear of the Herzogin Geila, for Gozbert, the Herzog, has died this night."

"Then may the Lord have mercy on us!" said the old man, adding softly, "In the world ye shall have tribulation."

CHAPTER 2

GISILHAR OF THE ARCH

But the prince of the kingdom of Persia withstood me one and twenty days: but, lo, Michael, one of the chief princes, came to help me; and I remained there with the kings of Persia. —Daniel 10:13

The Abbot-Bishop of Wirzburg—but what is an abbot-bishop? We have introduced the reader to unknown regions, and cannot proceed without explanation. Colman at Hochheim, and David at Wirzburg, as also Killean, their predecessor, were called abbots (*abbas*, that is, "fathers"), each being the guide of one of those missionary bands, consisting of twelve brethren and their families, who left Ireland in order to found settlements in Germany for the conversion of the heathen inhabitants. But David, the abbot of his own Irish brethren, was also the bishop, that is, pastor or shepherd, of the German converts gathering round the settlement. The terms "abbot" and "bishop" should not mislead the reader. The ancient Churches of Ireland and Scotland had little or nothing in common with the Roman Catholics of later times. Britain had been blessed with the Gospel as early as the third century, in the time of the Severan persecution. A Church had sprung up, and of the fervent men it produced, the two, perhaps, who did most for its development on the apostolic foundation, as well as for the spreading of the truth beyond their own land, were Ninian and Patrick, in the early part of the fifth century. To the untiring missionary zeal of the men of God, the German people in a great measure owe their conversion to Christianity. This Irish-Scottish Church did not practice celibacy. Its ministers (called "presbyters," which name later on grew into the appellation "priest"), as well as those who, as abbots, presided over a missionary settlement and the brethren who had gone out as co-messengers with the abbot, were, as a rule, married men.

The priests of the Irish Church considered it lawful to marry as late as the twelfth and thirteenth century, and knew no difference between secular clergy and monks. Those who, as Killean, for instance, and his fellow-messengers, went forth to the heathen, called themselves monachi, that is "men of solitude," not because they were without their lawfully wedded wives or shut up in monasteries, but because they lived separated from their own Church among the heathen. Their families had gone out with them, and their "solitude" consisted of separate cabins, one for each family, round the place of worship, and a common refectory. They were, moreover, in constant intercourse with the world around them, traveling to and fro in the prosecution of their missionary labors.

When a congregation had been formed of the converts, the abbot either himself was its bishop—that is, pastor—or he appointed one of his brethren to the office; in which case the bishop was subordinate to the abbot, who continued as chief guide of the settlement. All these abbots, in their turn, had a spiritual head in the Abbot of Iona, the ancient island-church on the west coast of Scotland. Such a mission station was called a cenoby, i.e., a place where persons live in community, but never a cloister or monastery. Records are extant, giving trustworthy information concerning these Irish mission settlements, or cenobies. Their center was always the church, or oratory. What these were like may be seen from specimens which have survived, as for instance at Devenish and Clondolkain, near Dublin, and another on the Flannan Isles.

Such an oratory consisted of a round massive stone tower, terminating in a high cupola[9]. A circular niche, opening out from the central nave[10], contained the simple communion table. The cupola served as a belfry[11].

Each of the brethren took share in the gospel work, and their wives were occupied in teaching, beside their own children, such of the heathen as could be gathered into schools. It would for this reason have been inconvenient if each wife had had the duty of house-keeping besides. The common refectory obviated this necessity, the simple meal consisting chiefly of vegetables, fish, or occasionally game.

Among the twelve brethren were generally some not ordained to the sacred work, but who, as serving brethren, with the help of the growing youths or some of the converts, provided for temporal needs—cultivating the fields, tending the cattle, cutting down trees for fuel, and the like. An island, either on a lake, or between the arms of some river, was a much-favored site, affording protection against the sudden attack of hostile heathen, but where such could not be found, the mission station was surrounded by a ring-fence. The converts usually settled round the cenoby, gradually forming new congregations. Those among them who were found fit, were trained for the ministry or presbytership, in order to assist or, as the case might be, replace the original twelve brethren, or to be sent out, that new cenobies might be founded. Some of these cenobies grew to be towns. Wurzburg, on the Main, for instance—as Hamelburg and Arnstadt in Germany, and St. Gall and Glarus in Switzerland—owes its existence to those Irish founders. Strassburg and Salzburg also are indebted to them.

Divine service was conducted in the simplicity of the ancient Church. There were no priestly vestments, no saint worship, no images; the language used always that of the converted people, the great aim being to diffuse the knowledge of the Bible. In keeping with their mission work, and, moreover, according to the practice of the early Church, was their habit of baptizing their own children, like those of heathen parents, not till after they had been instructed in the Christian faith.

Thus Bellaheld had completed her seventeenth year when she was deemed prepared for baptism on Easter Day, the 8th of April, 703.

On Easter Eve, when Abbot-Bishop David gathered the candidates about him to impress them once more with the sacred import of the intended act, his voice had a tremulous tenderness, and he concluded with these words: "Be not slothful in your part, examining yourselves earnestly, and humbly praying for the grace of the Spirit, that the Lord may find you well prepared, if it be His holy will that we should carry out what we have set before us. Be it according to His will!"

Most of the candidates did not understand why he should have added an "if." What should prevent their being baptized? One only of the young Christians knew the Abbot's meaning, a youth of the Herzog's household, named Haimerich. For it had been he who had whispered news to the Abbot which had filled the latter with the gravest apprehension.

"Something has happened to the Herzog," said Haimerich. "He was found senseless in his chamber. One of the serving women told us that, as she was setting supper in the hall, the Herzogin had suddenly risen from her seat, following a man-at-arms to the bed-chamber. That much is certain, and almost directly afterwards Pillung was dispatched to call home our Lord Hedan, who is away hunting the wild boar. I happened to stand by the door when the Herzogin passed, and she looked at me with terrible eyes. But our brother, the noble Gisilhar, charged me to tell you that he intended to be with you speedily."

The news was soon to be corroborated. As the Herzog was taking off his armor of buffalo hide, he was seized with apoplexy[12]. His frightened attendant hastened to call the Herzogin, who sat weaving with her women. They laid Gozbert upon the bed. His right side was paralyzed, and the power of speaking gone. Vainly he tried to express his desire that the Abbot should be sent for to pray with him. Geila knew well enough what he meant, but instead of sending for the Abbot she sent for the priest of Phol, a divinity which was supposed to reside in a grove close by. The Abbot, though unbidden, had no sooner parted with his young charges than he directed his steps to the Burg, to attend to the Herzog's spiritual need, but, reaching the entrance gate, he met the priest arriving from the other side with a hand-full of holy grasses, and with him Hezzilo, the chief priest of Woden, followed by a boy leading a goat destined to be sacrificed. The heathen priests were admitted, whereas the Abbot was refused entrance; the Herzog was asleep, he was told, and could not be disturbed.

With a heavy heart the aged servant of Christ had descended the hill and called together the brethren to prayer. They were on their knees in the oratory, and so absorbed in prayer that a young man entered unnoticed. He had a noble warlike figure; tall and stately. His eyes were blue, his fair hair long and curly. His powerful breast was coated with the usual armor of padded buffalo skin; the legs being cased in greaves[13] of hard leather, while spurs of bronze were fixed to his boots. A heavy iron sword in a wooden sheath completed his accoutrements. His helmet of buffalo hide was adorned with three heron feathers.

He had entered softly and knelt down, joining in the Abbot's prayers. The brethren did not notice him, till his loud "amen" mingled with theirs, when the Abbot turned to him almost precipitately, taking him by the hand and saying, "Gisilhar, what news?"

"Bad news," answered the young man. "That our God-fearing Herzog has had a stroke, thou knowest already, and the pagan priests, speedily sent for by the Herzogin Geila, thou hast seen with thine own eyes. I also saw them from the guest chamber as they entered the inner court by the light of torches, and I saw that Geila herself led Hezzilo to the dining hall. I was deeply grieved that this servant of darkness should trouble the dying man with his abominations, and followed him on the spot. The Herzogin shot a wrathful glance at me when I entered. She had already brought him to the door of the bed chamber, but I would not be deterred.

" 'Lady,' said I, 'what are you about? The Herzog is a Christian, and while he lives, his will is paramount, and not another's; not yours. And that it cannot be his will to have his dying hour polluted with devil's work you know full well. Away, thou servant of the evil one, get thee gone to thine own wicked altar! We care not how many goats and boars thou killest there, but thou shalt not hinder the Herzog departing in peace to his Lord and Master!' With these words I took the leering coward by the neck and turned him from the house."

"Thou hast dared much," said the Abbot. "Geila's wrath will be upon thee when the Herzog is gone."

"He is gone," continued Gisilhar. "His soul fled while I knelt with him, praying. As for the Herzogin I fear her not. She is not ruler of the land, but her son Hedan."

"Her influence with Hedan is great," replied the Abbot. "Were it not so, Hedan would have come to be baptized long ago."

"I know," said Gisilhar, "and if she had her way your work among the Thuringians would soon be stopped. But I have taken care of that. Seeing the Herzog had not long to live, I called three Christian and three heathen freemen to his bedside. Addressing him in their presence, and in the hearing of his wife I said, 'Herzog Gozbert, if it be that you understand my words, and in proof that your reason has not left you, lift up your left hand and place it upon this cross.'

"Whereupon his left hand took hold of the cross I held up before him, his right hand being powerless. Again I asked, 'Is it your dying will that Hedan, your son, shall be Herzog after you? Then testify to it by once more putting your hand upon the cross.' He did so. I continued, 'If it be your last will and command, that your son Hedan, as lord of the land when you are gone, shall leave the men of God to continue your holy work in peace, hindering or troubling them nowise, I ask you for a third time to take hold of the cross, and, if you are able, confirm your desire with a 'yes." And behold, the power of God so moved him that with both hands he seized the cross, and with clear voice spoke an unmistakable 'yes!'

"Thereupon I charged the witnesses, making the three Christian men swear by the cross, and the three heathen by their god Woden, that they would testify to what they had now seen and heard, and that they would stand by their testimony before the new Herzog and all the people to the end of their lives. Having thus put them to the oath, I brought them away with me to my own guest chamber, that by the right of hospitality I might protect them from the evil woman until Hedan should return."

"The Lord bless thee for what thou hast done!" said the Abbot, "but I tremble for thy life."

"Have no fears for me, father," replied Gisilhar. "I am no Thuringian, and owe them no allegiance. I am a free chieftain of the Bohmer Wald, and have come hither, as thou knowest, representing the free lords of the forest in the common cause against the Chawari. Geila knows she dare not harm me, and if she should yet venture, she would have to answer for it to the Herzogs of Bavaria, who are our true allies and Christian lords withal. As much as the Reginsburg[14], the grand old Roman fastness, out-towers this poor little Wirtsburg, so much also the power of Theudo and his sons outshines the power of Hedan, for they own the land far beyond the Danube, from the Fichtelberg in the north to the springs of the Isar and the Salzacha in the south."

"And thou gloriest in thy allegiance to Theudo," said the Abbot.

"Allegiance!" returned Gisilhar, almost angrily. "Have I not told thee I am a free lord on my own land in the forest? On the High Arch is built the house of my fathers, looking proudly upon the valley. If an enemy threatens the land, and the Herzog calls upon the free men to join in defense, then I too follow the call, but allegiance I owe him none."

"Thou owest thanks to the enemy, then, for having given thee occasion to go to Reginsburg, where thou madest the acquaintance of the holy man Rupert, who brought thee to the knowledge of God!"

"I do. It was five years ago when we joined arms against the Chawari. You know that Rupert is no Scotchman?"

"He is a Frank by birth; Worms on the Rhine is his home. He was a pupil at the cenoby which our Scottish brethren founded at Worms. It is just about seven years now since he went out from them with twelve fellow messengers to continue the work which Abbot-Bishop Erhard had begun at Reginsburg some twenty years before."

The venerable Abbot was thus conversing with the noble youth, when the notes of a buffalo horn sounded powerfully from the top of the mount.

"It is the watchman's notice that Hedan has arrived!" cried Gisilhar. "Let me return quickly, lest the Herzogin circumvent my precaution."

Hedan, having reached the inner court, leapt from his foaming charger, and forthwith entered the great hall, which, together with the retiring chamber already mentioned, formed the central part of the Wirtsburg. The dismal glow of torchlight but half dispelled the darkness of the place, the ceiling and wooden paneling of which were as black as untold years of smoke could make them. Hedan's looks went searching for his mother. He scarcely recognized the motionless figure which, on a low seat by the idle loom, sat staring into vacancy, paying no heed to his arrival.

"How goes it with my father?" cried Hedan. The figure rose noiselessly and, gliding before him, opened the door to the chamber of death.

"He is gone!" cried Hedan, with fearful emotion.

"He is dead," reiterated his mother with icy coldness, "and thou art the Herzog. But another has forestalled thy orders."

"Who has dared it?" exclaimed the young ruler, with rising passion. "Who dared disregard my power?"

"Thy hands have been tied," said Geila bitterly. "Gisilhar of the Arch took it upon himself to mark out the way thou shouldest go."

"He dared it!" cried Hedan wrathfully. "Who is he, to play the lord here? He shall answer me with the sword."

"Listen to me first. He has made sure of six witnesses, who will swear to thee, three of them by Woden, and three by the Crucified One they call their God, that thy father, just before his death, had raised his hand in affirmation, when Gisilhar asked him whether it was his last will and command to thee, to let these strangers continue their work unscathed. For Gisilhar, in putting the question to him, told him to do so. He understood that much, but the purport of the question was beyond him, I say."

"And what else is of Gisilhar's ordering?" asked Hedan frowningly.

"What elsc? Is not that enough?" returned his mother.

"Well, he is a Christian!" said Hedan. "He could not but try to prevent any harm that might befall these men of God."

"He has dared to order people about here as though he were master," continued Geila. "He introduced these six retainers[15] into the retiring chamber, which hitherto has been sacred to any foot save thy father's and mine. And, not satisfied with this, he shut them up in the guest chamber, where they are at this moment. As for me, he kept me away from my dying husband. It was he who received his last breath, not I. But there he is himself. I hear him coming, and his six witnesses with him. Take heed, Hedan, to receive him with due reverence for he will expect it of thee."

Gisilhar entered, the six retainers following.

"Go about your business till I require your attendance!" said Hedan sharply to the latter. Then turning to his guest, he added coldly, "You might have spared yourself the trouble, Sir Gisilhar! That it was my father's desire to leave the Hibernians unmolested I know full well, without your witnesses—"

"Quite so," interrupted Gisilhar. "He affirmed this his last will and command by lifting both his hands, and by a clear, 'yes.' I am convinced, noble Herzog, that you will honor his dying will and act upon it."

"Just so," said Hedan. "I will honor his will no more or less than he honored his father's last desire. Did not his dying father bid him to remain faithful to our gods? And did he act upon it? Since when, Sir Gisilhar, is it meet that the dying Herzog should prescribe for the heir of his power? If it is my pleasure to persecute the strangers and destroy their worship, you will not hinder it by your six witnesses. It is not my pleasure. I desire rather to leave them in peace, not because my father has thus enjoined me, but because I consider it well and prudent. If you had kept yourself from interference, I would not have hurt a hair of their heads, but, because you have presumed to play the lord here, administering oaths to my retainers, introducing them into my mother's very bed-chamber, I will let you and them find out who is master here."

"Conard," he said, turning to one of his men, "go down to the Abbot forthwith and charge him to have no bell-ringing, no psalm-singing, no worship of any kind for a month to come, because of my father's death. I'll just see if they will not obey me as their lord! And tell him it is my intention to take charge myself of my father's funeral rites in the forest. We shall not require their assistance. As for you, Sir Gisilhar of the Arch, I might well turn you from my board for having abused of hospitality. I will not do it. For the sake of Herzog Theudo, who has sent you, you may stay as long as you please."

"I shall not please to make further use of your hospitality, most noble Herzog," said Gisilhar proudly. "Nor was it my intention to tie your hands, but rather to free them." He stepped from the hall, ordered his men to saddle the horses, and rode off.

Day was breaking. As he reached the cenoby, he found the little colony in great consternation. Conard had just delivered his message. "We cannot obey this injunction!" exclaimed several of the younger brethren. "It is the will of God that we worship Him this Easter Day, and we should obey God rather than men!"

"See that ye mistake not His will," said the Abbot. "It is written nowhere in His word that we should ring the Easter bell. When St. Paul was a prisoner at Rome, he did not keep the days of unleavened bread with the brethren. He did not say, 'It is the will of God I should; let me burst from my prison and keep Easter time,' but he worshipped the Lord in bonds. Thus ye also are His prisoners now, not shut in and fettered, but shut out from your oratory. Go, then, to your cabins and worship Him in silence; ay, and in tears, if perchance the Lord will turn the heart of the new Herzog and give him thoughts of peace toward us. And, indeed, it is by humble obedience that we shall gain most. If we defy this grievous command, the work will suffer."

Gisilhar shared this opinion, and the brethren resolved to obey Hedan's behest. Bellaheld and the rest of the candidates, therefore, could not be baptized for another month, if then. When Bellaheld learned this, she said sadly, "Could I but go to my mother! Brother Heddo has just brought me word from Hochheim that she is sick unto death, and not likely to live another day."

The Abbot, hearing this, was anxious she should go, but knew of no safeguard to escort her.

"I do," rejoined Gisilhar. "All the more as it is my intention not to leave the country without bidding farewell to our brethren at Hochheim. If the maiden will trust herself to me, I will take her thither in safety."

A saddle horse being provided for her, the maiden set out with Gisilhar, followed by his two servants, old Trudpert and curly-headed Dado.

The rising sun had crowned the hills with a purple glory. But Bellaheld's tearful eyes sought the ground. She thought of her mother, and the world was dark to her. She was glad to see her once more, but the sorrow of this last meeting far outweighed any joy. It was a disappointment to her also to return unbaptized. She rode along in mournful silence, and Gisilhar, whose eyes could not but be charmed with his lovely charge, dared not disturb her grief. His two servants, however, to while away the time, presently fell into a loud conversation, beginning to tell each other mysterious tales of the various divinities worshipped by their neighbors—of Woden among others.

Gisilhar, hearing it, turned around. "Trudpert," said he reprovingly, "how often have I told thee not to speak thus lightly of the devil?"

"Is Woden the devil?" asked Bellaheld.

Gisilhar was taken by surprise, but said after a while, "I met a priest one day who had come from beyond the Alps, and he assured me that the best means of making the people turn against their heathen gods was to tell them that these were just the devil and his angels who war against the kingdom of light. It seemed to me good counsel."

"But it is not true," said the maiden. "It cannot be right to say what is not true."

"Does not St. Paul tell us that the things which the Gentiles sacrifice, they sacrifice to devils?"

"He also says that an idol is nothing. Judge for thyself. Is there a Woden?"

"Certainly not."

"But there is a prince of darkness, the chief of fallen angels. We know it is deception to tell men there is a Woden. Worshipping him also is deception, which pleases him who is the father of lies. But if thou tellest thy servant, 'Woden himself is the father of lies and the prince of darkness,' thou mayest be guilty of great wrong. For hitherto he has thought of Woden as an old man with a beard of lichen, riding on a white horse, and sometimes on the wind, chasing his faithless wife, and he will be likely to turn the adversary of Christ

Jesus into just such a silly ghost. And if the men of God tell him, 'There is no Woden,' and thou addest, 'Woden is the devil,' how should he not come to imagine the teachings of the Scriptures no better than the heathen tales of Woden and the like?"

"Thou art right," exclaimed Gisilhar, looking at his companion with undisguised surprise. To tell the truth, he had taken little notice of her so far. That she was fair to behold, he could not but see, but beyond this he saw in her merely a maiden entrusted to his care, and one greatly beneath him in position. Now, to his astonishment, he found her a woman to be listened to. Her sad face lit up as she spoke, a wondrous light breaking from her eyes. She was indeed beautiful to behold and he could not but own the majestic loveliness of her whole bearing.

"Father David has told me," she continued, "that these transalpine[16] priests are teaching a strange mixture of truth and falsehood, bewildering the people in Britain, whither they have taken the Gospel. In order to gain the heathen in greater masses, they allow them to keep some of their pagan conceits, changing the names perhaps, but condoning the practices. Instead of praying to God, as Christians have done since the Church's earliest time, they call upon saints and martyrs themselves, asking for their intercession in our behalf. Instead of idols, they have saints now, offering them worship in heathen fashion. The name only is changed. Idolatry has remained, and the latter abomination is greater than the former, because it pretends to be Christian. The very sacrifices have remained under the guise of Christian festivals. Our men of God, who hate such a mixing of heathen practice and Christian teaching, who are not satisfied with what is half-and-half, and will not admit a man to baptism unless he has truly repented himself of his sins and turned to the Lord with a whole heart, have much to suffer from those priests of the Roman Church. They affect to despise our abbots and bishops because, like the Apostles, they live in holy wedlock. The Bishop of Rome himself insists on what is nowhere taught in the Bible, as though it were a sin in a minister of the Church to have a wife."

"What a foolish craze!" exclaimed Gisilhar. "To be sure," continued he, but stopped short. "To be sure," he was going to say, "if marriage were not interdicted[17] in our Irish cenobies also, one need not fear lest one of the brethren should take a maiden to wife who might well delight a man's heart, and whom I would fain gain for myself." But he considered that Bellaheld was on the way to her mother's deathbed, and suppressed the thought.

Yet, knowing he might possibly not meet her again for a long time, he could not help letting her see indirectly what he dared not put into clearer words. "The men of God," he said after a while, "are not forbidden, I believe, to look for a wife beyond their own cenoby?"

"Oh, no!" replied Bellaheld. "They may marry whom they please, only of course not heathen girls. Their wives must be true, zealous, and humble-minded Christians. Brother Huckbald, for instance, has married one of our converts, and found in her a God-fearing wife and a faithful helpmeet in his holy vocation."

"And I suppose," said Gisilhar, "the men of God would not necessarily expect their daughters to wed a brother within the cenoby, but one of them might follow a Christian husband to his home beyond, if she were so minded. Indeed I remember," he added, "that only last year a daughter of our venerable Abbot Rupert, at Reginsburg, married a Bavarian husband of Herzog Theudo's household. If we might suppose now that sooner or later a freeman, whose home is neither at Hochheim nor at Wirzburg, should turn hither the steps of his charger, hoping to gain Bellaheld for his wife, and, if she were not loath to accept him, there would be no reason why the two should not be joined in happy wedlock? But," he continued, as the maiden blushingly averted her face, "this is no time for such fancies. It is not lover's music, but sounds of mourning which ring in thine ear. I pray the Lord in His mercy to spare thy mother, to grant her the joy of assisting at thy baptism, and to grant me the happiness of knowing the mother of such a daughter!"

"Let it be according to His will!" said Bellaheld gently, the tears falling from her eyes.

Gisilhar was silent. His secret thought turned to fervent prayer. If that prayer could be heard, Bellaheld's mother would be brought back from the gates of death, and he would not hide from her the wish of his heart. She herself should gain him the daughter's acceptance, and the mother's hand would bless him who, in future, would be her son, and the rightful protector of her darling child.

As his thoughts were thus running on apace, the woodland opened out before them. Another turn and Hochheim lay open to their view. Gisilhar felt his heart beat, but poor Bellaheld's was ready to stand still.

The solemn notes of the communion hymn rose from the oratory, carried on the wings of the wind. The gate of the ring-fence was closed and not unguarded, but the watchman knew the approaching maiden, and opened without delay. "It is well thou art come," he said. "Thy mother is at the point of death."

CHAPTER 3

A NOBLE SUITOR

He made his grave with the wicked... —Isaiah 53:9

Gisilhar did not see Bellaheld again. His sense of honor, as well as offended pride, urged him to quit Hedan's dominions as speedily as possible. He left that same afternoon to return to Bavaria. Bellaheld was kneeling by her mother's coffin. Of Gisilhar she thought no more.

The mortal remains of the faithful Mechild were taken to their last resting place amid the hymn-singing of the Christian people. But the congregation had need to put on the garb of mourning, for sorrow was gathering on the horizon.

"Geila's influence on Hedan is great," Abbot David had said to Gisilhar, and truly it was so. The latter's well-meaning interference by Gozbert's dying bed only served to make matters more easy for the evil-minded Herzogin. Hedan was irritated, and felt it a point of honor not to be advised by Gisilhar, whom he watched riding off with the satisfaction of having shown him the door. But his feelings of dislike to the meddling stranger found vent in a growing hatred of the Hibernian settlers in general, for were they not of the same faith with Gisilhar and his trusted friends? The old Herzogin had no difficulty in making Hedan believe Gisilhar, after all, had only carried out what had been carefully planned in the cenoby. But he would hold his own!

On Easter morning, two of the Herzog's men, fully armed, arrived at the door of the oratory to keep watch that none of the Christians should think of entering the sanctuary. Geila, of course, had chosen two heathen for the office, Pillung and Morung by name. They brought a hamper of game with them and a large cask of beer to fill up the time between the singing of coarse heathen songs. Their noise was such that the brethren could not even worship in their own cabins, which none dared leave. In the evening two other spies relieved guard, and their noise was, if possible, still greater. The oratory continued closely watched.

In the course of the week, the funeral of Herzog Gozbert took place. Not in the least considering the fact that he had been a Christian, it was, under Geila's direction, performed according to heathen rites. A pyre was raised in the forest, and the corpse in full armor was carried thither by the departed Herzog's favorite steed. Geila and her women followed with wild lamentation. Behind them was Hedan, surrounded by all his men-at-arms; even the Christians among them having been obliged to take part in the ceremony.

As the procession went through the beech forest, Haimerich stepped to the side of the young Herzog, boldly addressing him: "What do you expect the gods will do with your father's soul? They cannot admit him to Walhalla[18]. Were they true, they would have to send him to Hel[19]."

"Insolent churl!" exclaimed Hedan, but could add no more, for the reasoning of his Christian retainer was too obvious to be denied.

Haimerich coolly continued, "You have made but poor provision for the departed Herzog. Our Abbot would have done better. He would have recommended him to the mercy of God who made heaven and earth, that, by the merit of Christ Jesus, he might enter paradise."

Hedan looked to the ground in sulky silence. "My mother insisted on it," he said presently. "It is her doing, not mine. Tell the Abbot he shall pray for my father's soul." He waved his hand, and Haimerich, obeying the sign, left his side.

The procession had arrived at the funeral pyre. Hezzilo, the priest of Woden, stood in readiness with his attendants to receive the corpse. But no sooner had Haimerich caught sight of the ministers of darkness than he turned on his heels, followed by all those among the men who were Christians. Heedless of permission, they returned by the way they had come. Hedan did not call them back. It was the lesser number who remained behind. When Geila noticed the defection, they were disappearing between the beeches. "What are they about?" she exclaimed angrily.

"I have sent them on a message to the Abbot," replied Hedan. "My father, having been a Christian, will not find admittance with the gods. The Abbot may as well pray for him to his God, else his soul will remain homeless."

"Foolish prate!" retorted Geila. "He was my husband, and the gods will receive him."

"Hel shall receive him!" answered the strange voice of a Druidess, appearing suddenly before the horrified Herzogin, as though risen out of the earth. The weird figure seemed of gigantic size, as she screamed with glaring eyes and wildly streaming hair. "Does Geila think the gods favor her because she is the Herzogin? I tell thee, they will not receive thy wicked husband. There is no forgiveness with the gods. They will give him his portion with the children of Loki; the serpent Iormungander will hold him fast; the Fenrirwolf will gnaw away his heart; the wild Hel will rejoice at his misery!"

"Hold thy peace, Walda!" interrupted Hezzilo. "Did I not enjoin thee to keep aloof? Wherefore comest thou to disturb the holy rite?"

"Thou didst tell me," cried the Druidess, "but imaginest thou that Walda is frightened away by an artful priest, when the voice of god is within her?"

"It is an ill-advised god that speaks from thee," replied the priest, trying to cover his confusion with an appearance of confidence. "Thou knowest not that Gozbert repented on his deathbed and returned to the gods of his fathers. Thou knowest not that by his own command I am here to celebrate the sacrifice and offer up the favorite horse to all-powerful Woden. How shouldest thou know that Pillung, secretly following Gisilhar, the stranger, heard him tell the Abbot that the dying Herzog would not listen to his prayer, but asked for me, the priest of Woden? Return to thy cave, Walda! I know thou meanest well, and, thinking Gozbert had died a Christian, thou hast come, lest the service of Woden be profaned. No, it was no god that spoke from thee, but the voice born of thine own thought."

The Druidess retired sullenly. "What is this about Pillung?" asked Geila and Hedan, amazed.

"He can speak for himself," said the wily priest. And Pillung, stepping forward, affirmed the false tale, making use of fearful oaths. He had been carefully instructed by Hezzilo, whose hatred of Gisilhar knew no bounds.

He was in truth a cunning man, this priest of Woden. He knew the Herzog had died a Christian, and that complying with Geila's request to conduct the funeral according to heathen rites was really a profanation of the worship which he pretended to hold sacred. Walda's fanatical imprecations at least were honest. But the crafty priest considered that nothing would be more hurtful to the cause of heathenism than his refusing to receive the body of the departed Herzog, and that nothing would be more likely to injure the growth of Christianity than to re-establish, at the Herzog's funeral, the religion which he had banished from the Wirtsburg. This was a triumph not to be foregone. To make it possible, he invented the tale, prevailing upon Pillung to swear to it falsely. The most immediate gain was this, that any latent desire in Hedan's breast to honor his father's dying will was effectually stifled. Or rather, Hedan now consoled himself that his father's dying wish had been the very opposite from what Gisilhar had tried to adduce by his witnesses. Gozbert had evidently changed his mind after they had left him. Had not Pillung affirmed his testimony with the direst oaths, raising his right hand and saying, "If it be not as I say, let Woden crush this my right hand which I lift to him!"

The ceremony proceeded without further interruption. The corpse was placed on the pyre, tied upright in a sitting posture. The favorite horse of the deceased, a milk-white charger, was killed by Hezzilo, and also laid upon the pile. It was soon ablaze, burning up the corpses of the late Herzog and his steed, while the priests walked round it with dismal dirges. The flames rose to the height of the beech tops, and the suffocating stench was carried by the west wind far into the valley of the Main. When the pile had sunk down to ashes, the remaining heap was covered with earth and turf. The sword-blade and other bits of metal outlasting the fire were buried separately.

When the procession moved homeward, Geila triumphed in her heart. The story told by Hezzilo and sworn to by Pillung, that Gozbert had recanted just before his death, was most eagerly received by her. She believed it because it suited her. She herself had been present, seeing and hearing, when the dying Herzog testified to his desire that the men of God should be left unmolested. She had seen him raise his hands; she had heard the "yes" of the paralyzed man. And when the six witnesses had left him, she had remained in the chamber, sitting apart, but seeing and hearing that Gisilhar offered up prayer by the bedside. It is true that she could not follow the words, but, on the other hand, she had seen nothing that could have led her to believe the dying man had interrupted the prayer. Indeed, she knew it was scarcely possible that he should have spoken again after that "yes" which, in itself, was almost miraculous, for Gisilhar had not been praying many minutes when the breathing became heavier, sinking away presently into the silence of death. Geila knew all this, and yet she held herself assured of the contrary, for had not Pillung sworn to it? Had he not heard Gisilhar confess to the Abbot that Gozbert had called for Hezzilo, had prayed to Woden? Surely it must be so. It was not her fault if, sitting apart, she had not heard his dying word.

This unexpected disclosure had greatly delighted her. It was a triumph indeed, and she spoke of it to Hedan all the way home. Yet she could not get rid of a secret fear to which the sinking shadows of the night added mystery.

After supper, Hedan retired to his own abode in the side wing beyond the court, and Geila, not without a shudder, entered the chamber in which Gozbert had breathed his last. She went to rest, but sleep fled her couch. As often as she closed her eyes, she fancied she heard her husband gasping in death, and jumped up affrighted. It was turned midnight when at last she slept, but only to be wakeful in dreams.

Towards morning, when the rising moon cast a pale glimmer through the trellised window, lighting up the empty place beside her, she started. Was she dreaming? Was she waking? She thought she saw Gozbert beside her, lifting both hands towards the cross. Terrified, she closed her eyes and listened whether he would call for Hezzilo, but Gisilhar prayed an endless prayer, and she slept. Now she wandered in dreams through the forest, looking for the pile of ashes, but could not find it. Now to her right, now to her left, she caught sight of Haimerich leading the little band of Christians back to the Wirtsburg. She would have flown after them wrathfully, but her feet obeyed her not: in vain tried she to move, when suddenly Walda burst from the thicket wildly screaming, "Hel has received him!" and Geila awoke.

She would have influenced Hedan to anything, had she been able. At her bidding he would have chased the Hibernians from his dominions, and would have forced his Christian subjects to offer sacrifice to Woden. But Geila, waking, seemed paralyzed, as her feet had been in her dreams. Listless, she sat in the great hall, mute and brooding. Her son attributed it to the grief of widowhood. As far as he was concerned, he never for a moment doubted the story he had been told. It was plain that his father had, at the very last, returned to the gods. Gisilhar had told him an untruth, and Gisilhar had been the mouthpiece of the cenoby. The pious brethren must be punished. If Hedan did not set about this meditated punishment with a high hand, but bided his time for aggrieving the holy men, it was only that, knowing his mother's feelings in this respect, he felt sure of losing nothing if he waited for her instigation. If she was satisfied to leave the strangers in peace a few days longer, he could be. Of one thing he was firmly resolved: the worship of the strange god should not again be heard in his land; no singing, no sound of bells should rise again from the oratories.

Consequently, on the Saturday after Easter, he said to his mother, "I cannot permit service at Hochheim any more than here. I will ride over this very morning and stop it."

Geila looked at him wondering. A gleam of satisfaction broke from her eyes. "Good fortune speed thee, my son!" she cried as he called for his horse and rode from the Burg.

Geila had come to herself again, now in her right mind. Hedan was acting on his own responsibility; what need she fear? He was Herzog and ruler of the land. She could leave matters with him. She rose from her seat and watched her son's departure till, having crossed the river on a ferry, he vanished in the forest.

"He is a noble hero," she said. "The spirit of his ancestor is upon him, whose name he bears, and the spirit of Hruod, the first of our race. He will purify the land of these foreign offenders, and will restore the worship of the mighty gods, of Woden and Thor, of Phol and Eor. He has taken a weight from my mind. It is not his mother's counsel he needs. But he needs a wife. It is not meet that I continue in the retiring chamber, leaving him to abide in the wing. My hair has grown white with years. It is meet for me to accept the lot of widowhood. Let him bring a blooming wife to the hall. But he shall not think of wedding a daughter of the Bavarian Herzog who has listened to the strangers and forsworn the gods. Horsa, the Saxon ruler, has a daughter of whom I have heard wondrous tales. At the hour of her birth, her father killed ten men and twenty women, offering them up to Friga. The goddess accepted the sacrifice, blessing the maid with beauty and strength withal. As touched by sunbeams are Irminfrid's auburn curls. She is tall, and sits her horse like a hero. She hunts the elk and the dread aurochs[20], and throws the millstone farther than our finest men. Of her I will speak to Hedan, that he may go and take her to wife, and a valiant race shall be born of them."

As Geila was thus giving her fancy the rein, Hedan rode moodily through the arching aisles of beech of an all-but-virgin forest. The grand old trees were breaking into the first tender foliage of spring. Here and there some mighty giant, uprooted by the winter storms, lay half-buried in the leafy mould, moss growing wherever it had a chance, and the underwood clothing itself with multitudinous buds. The beams of the morning sun shone aslant through the interlacing boughs. Thousands of birds were singing, and a bittern, starting from a sheet of water close by, flew up with a far-sounding call. A doe looked at the rider from behind an elder bush, letting him approach to within twenty steps when she bounded away gaily. A black squirrel ran up the trunk of a beech, turning round on the first bough to look slyly at the young man beneath. He laughed and held out a hand to the merry-eyed creature, but it sped away from branch to branch to the topmost retreat and vanished from his pursuing gaze.

Then he examined the track of a stag which crossed his path, and once more turned his looks aloft, delighting in the sunbeams overhead and watching a pair of thrushes as they caroled round their nest. He had quite forgotten that he was on his way to silence songs of another kind. He opened his heart entirely to the influences of that early spring.

But, hark! There was an echo floating through the forest deeps like a distant harmony. It was the bell of the oratory at Hochheim, calling the brethren to matins[21]. Wondrously pure was the silver cadence borne to him on the air. It was no unknown sound. Hedan had heard it many a morning in his father's lifetime who, in years gone by, had often taken the boy by the hand to follow the invitation, and Hedan, by his father's side, had listened with awe to the sacred strains within the oratory. The melodious peal, greeting him as he rode towards Hochheim, did, therefore, not surprise him. It seemed, on the contrary, a very part of the beauteous morning. The youthful Herzog could not but stop his horse and listen. The calling bell had never seemed so lovely before. He continued listening, almost dreaming, till, startled by a noisy jay, he bethought himself, remembering that these bells were ringing their own death knell, that he would never hear them again, being on his way to forbid them for ever.

He was startled by this aspect of his intentions. He stopped trying to disentangle his bewildered thoughts and feelings, but before he could recover his serenity, he was again disturbed. From behind a rock by the side of his path, moans arose so pitiful that he listened aghast. He turned his horse's head to discover the cause, and remained transfixed. A maiden of almost heavenly glory, dressed in ample folds of white, and lovely as Freia herself, was bending over a pale-faced man whose eyes were closed and whose forehead was streaming with blood. A phial of oil was in her hand. She was just about to dress and bind up the wound, but turned at the sudden noise, meeting Hedan's astonished look with a quiet gaze.

"Who art thou?" asked the bewildered Herzog, springing from his horse. "As a Valkyr[22] maiden thou appearest before me, about to carry a slain hero to Walhalla. Stay, and do not rise as a swan to disappear from my earthly sight!"

"I am no Valkyr maiden, as thou deemest," said the damsel. "I am Bellaheld, the daughter of Iberius, a man of God, who is no longer here."

"If thou art a mortal maid, how darest thou trust thyself alone in the forest?" asked the Herzog, gazing at her admiringly as she turned again to the wounded man to attend to his need.

"I am not alone," said Bellaheld. "God is with me, in whose service I came hither."

"In the service of God?" repeated Hedan, wonderingly. "Who is this man lying wounded before thee?

"I know him not," replied she, "but Damoalis believes he is the same Kathalt who, three days ago, tried to set fire to one of our cabins, so that the whole cenoby would have been destroyed had it not been for one of the brethren who was able to stifle the flame before it spread."

"And thou returnest good to one who wished you evil? How is it?"

"The boy Damoalis, who had gone to the wood to look for healing herbs, found him lying here wounded and half dead. He ran back to the cenoby to tell the brethren. The Abbot, hearing of it, sent me on at once to look to the poor man's wounds. Two of the brethren are following with a stretcher to take him to our hospice where he may be tended and recover, if it please God."

"The man who would have destroyed the cenoby?"

"Why should we hate him who hated us? He hates us because he is a poor heathen, thinking thereby to please his gods. But our God has told us to do good to them which hate us and despitefully use us."

"Bellaheld!" resumed the Herzog, evidently moved, "thou sayest thy God is present here—" he stopped, not knowing how to continue. When the storm went raging through the forest, shattering the fir trees and the mighty oaks which braved a thousand winters, then indeed the heathen said, "Woden is among us; Woden rides atop of the forest, followed by the ghostly hunt."

But there was no uproar now. The sacred stillness of the morning spoke of peace only, when a tender maiden could enter securely the lonely haunt, showing mercy to one who hated her people and was an enemy to her faith! Hedan felt the breath of a Spirit; of a God higher than Woden. He could not express what he felt, and only repeated, "Thou sayest thy God is present here!"

"He is," said the maiden reverently, "and it is He who brought you here, most noble Herzog."

"Dost thou know me?" queried Hedan in surprise.

"How should I not, having often seen you pass the cenoby at Wirzburg?"

"And it is thy God, thinkest thou, who brought me? Canst thou say also for what purpose He brought me?"

"To assist me with this poor sufferer; that you should lift him upon your horse and take him to the cenoby. He is weak with loss of blood. The brethren, having first to prepare a stretcher, cannot be here for some time yet."

And the Herzog did lift the wounded man, Kathalt, in

his strong arms, mounting the horse behind him. It was strange he should thus approach the cenoby, actually doing the will of that God whose worship he had come to destroy. Bellaheld followed at an increasing distance.

"Who was it that thus wounded thee?" asked Hedan after a while of the man in his charge.

"Othmar," replied the latter. "We fell to blows over a roebuck which he claimed to have killed, although it was my booty."

"Why didst thou moan so pitifully, just as I approached the spot where the maiden was tending thee?"

"The woman hurt me, drawing the splinter from the wound."

"The woman!" repeated Hedan. "Canst thou not speak of thy mistress more reverently?"

"Is she my mistress?" asked Kathalt, wondering.

"She will be before long," said the Herzog, and was silent.

Bellaheld reached the cenoby some time after Hedan, and was surprised to see the old doorkeeper, Brother Faramund, not only step aside respectfully to let her pass, but bend his head before her, at the same time crossing his hands upon his breast as he would to the Abbot.

She passed him, marveling at his solemnity and sadness. When she reached the open place before the oratory, she found the whole of the little community standing about in somber groups. At this she scarcely wondered, the Herzog's presence within the cenoby, to her mind, being sufficient explanation. But no sooner had she herself been seen, then all turned towards her.

Her mother's friend, Gertrude, embraced her, and whispered in her ear, "Fear not, daughter of my friend, for God shall bear thee up."

The aged Totman, coming up, said, "Bellaheld, thou art wanted in the Abbot's cabin."

She turned obediently to do as she was bidden, wondering at Gertrude's greeting. The little wooden house, inhabited by Abbot Colman, was as simple and poor as any of the brethren's dwellings. When she entered, she saw Hedan standing by the side of the venerable Abbot.

"Bellaheld," said the latter, "the Herzog desires to speak to thee." She looked innocently at the young ruler.

"I have something to tell thee," said Hedan. "Amongst all of the fair maidens in this land, I have chosen thee alone to be my wife, the Herzogin, and in thy honor, I shall not further forbid the worship of thy god in this, my land. It is my command—nay, my heart's desire!"

Bellaheld answered not. A pallor had spread on her face, and, when Hedan had ended, she lay swooning in Totman's arms.

"Forgive her," said the old man. "It has taken her unawares. She is a tender maiden and lowly at heart. That you would have her be Herzogin has frightened her greatly. Bear with her for she will soon be herself again."

Totman carried her to the adjoining chamber where the Abbot's wife cooled her temples with water. Bellaheld opened her eyes wonderingly, and a word escaped her lips so softly none heard it—"Gisilhar!" she said.

"The Herzog has commanded a weighty thing, and I think he will not take refusal lightly," whispered Totman presently. "But Bellaheld, nor shouldest thou accept him lightly, though he be thy lawful ruler, for to marry the Herzog is to be unequally yoked, and to spend your days among heathens."

"I thank thee, Totman," the maiden said, "for what you

say is right. Fear not, I know my answer already."

She rose stiffly and left the chamber upright and strong. Hedan stood by the Abbot when the maiden came up to him and with a brave look in her eyes said, "Most noble Herzog, I fear I cannot accept your gracious offer, for my God has indeed said that believers are not to bind themselves with unbelievers." She looked at him steadily and his countenance changed. His expression became first thoughtful, then grim.

"So this is the way Christians obey their lawful rulers?" he returned. "This is how your God teaches you to obey?" He turned and walked a few paces.

"Nay, but it doth bid me to obey all lawful commands and to live at peace with all as I may," she replied.

The Herzog turned suddenly back to the maiden. He stood for a moment gathering his thoughts, and then he declared with a terrible calmness in his voice, "I tell thee, my lady, if thou dost not change thy resolution it will be much the worse for thee and all thy brethren! I shall leave here with a betrothed wife or there shall be great suffering on thy account!"

Here he stopped and, having spent the greater part of his anger, he waited to see the effects of his words.

Bellaheld stood torn by the decision in front of her. In an instant she remembered the words of our Savior who said, "Greater love hath no man than he lay down his life for his friend," and though her face had paled greatly, she gathered her courage and answered again.

"Most noble Herzog," she said, "if with your hand you will pledge me your word that all my brethren and sisters, both here and at Wirzburg, shall continue in their faith serving God, protected by yourself; if this be your honest will, it shall be as you have commanded it. I will be a true and faithful wife to you, honoring you as my husband. But remember, my God will even then be present with me."

Looking to the Abbot, she smiled bravely and before he could move to stop her, she swallowed the sobs in her throat, and tremblingly held out her hand. The Herzog, perceiving that his threats and commands had gotten him what he wanted, immediately smiled, and clasped her to his heart, then covered her hand with kisses.

CHAPTER 4

MOTHER AND WIFE

I will lead them in paths that they have not known: I will make darkness light before them, and crooked things straight. —Isaiah 42:16

The mid-day meal was waiting in the dim paneled hall, when Hedan jumped from his horse in the courtyard, throwing the bridle to an attendant. Pleasure glowed from his face as he entered, stepping at once to the dais at the upper part of the hall, where the table was spread for himself and his mother.

Geila looked at him no less delighted. "Right glad I am,"

she said, "that with a strong hand thou hast taken hold of the reins. Thou hast no need of my advice, and without fears I may retire in widowhood."

This sentiment met with more approval on the young ruler's part than his mother would have been pleased to know. Hedan smiled to himself as he carved the haunch of venison which had been set before him, but asked presently, with apparent unconcern, "Where dost thou propose to take up thy abode for the future? If I am not mistaken, my grandmother went to the Hamelburg when my father succeeded, did she not?"

This was more than the old Herzogin was pleased to hear. When she spoke of retiring, she meant to do so within the Wirtsburg, not to some lonely place miles and miles away. But, pride stepping in, she said, "I am ready to go whither the Herzog, my son, will send me."

"The Hamelburg," continued the latter, with perfect ease, "is in good condition, I believe. But this Wirtsburg must be thoroughly repaired before I can expect a wife to come to me. How low and dingy is this hall! Everything black and—"

"Thou art thinking of a wife!" exclaimed Geila, delighted. "The very thing I have wished for thee this morning! And truly she is a glorious maiden whom I have chosen to be thy bride. To Horsa, the Herzog of the Saxons, thou must go; his daughter, Irminfrid—"

"Thou shouldest have told me of her before," interrupted Hedan. "When my father was alive, you and he might have proposed the wife for me. Now I am lord paramount of the land. The Herzog will choose his bride for himself."

"But he will not spurn his mother's advice," replied she with a tone which well betrayed her secret anger, in spite of apparent gentleness.

"I have no need of thy advice. Thou saidst so but a moment since. Indeed, I have fixed my choice. In three weeks, when the days of mourning are over, I hope to lead home the lovely bride to whom I was brought, they say, by God."

The Herzogin looked at him speechless. "God? Which God?" she was going to ask, but could not, for Hedan continued pleasantly, "And much has to be done by then. I must send to Reginsburg for masons. They have far better houses there, having learnt of the Romans. Their walls are of stone, the ceilings plastered, and the floor not, as with us, of bare trodden-down soil, but covered with flags. In the sleeping chambers it is even boarded. Herzog Theudo also has panes of glass in his windows, instead of trellis-work. He procured them at great cost from beyond the Alps. I shall hardly be able to get the like, the time being short; however, I will try. If I cannot get glass, they have a transparent stone in Neustria, called moonstone, which will do as well."

Thus he went on till the venison and a dish of pike had been dispatched. Having risen from the table, he called to some of his retainers, who were dining in the lower part of the hall, giving them various commissions with regard to the plans just elaborated. But as he spoke, one of the men stepped forward, holding high a birch cup filled with frothy beer, and exclaimed, "Hail to the Herzog! Hail also to the chosen bride!"

The Herzog joined cups with him graciously, and, approaching the lower board amid the joyous acclamations of the men, he accepted the pledge of each of them. When he returned to the dais he found that his mother had left the hall.

"Haimerich!" commanded the Herzog, "follow me." The young man, thus called upon, attended his master to the little room in the wing above the stable, still occupied by Hedan. Having reached it, the latter began, "I told thee at the time of my father's funeral to request the Abbot's prayer for his soul. Now thou shalt go to him and say he may begin to worship again with bell-ringing and psalm-singing, just as in my father's lifetime."

Whereupon Haimerich folded his hands, exclaiming, "Blessed be Christ Jesus, the Heavenly Lord, who has guided your heart! I never doubted that you would come to honor your father's dying wish."

"Indeed, thou art mistaken," said Hedan, smiling pleasantly. "It is the first wish of my bride, rather than my father's last desire, which I thus carry into effect. My father's last desire, moreover, was not as thou deemest."

"Alas," said Haimerich, "that you should believe it! I have heard the tale concocted by Hezzilo and the drunken Pillung. If it were true, surely your own mother would have been the first to know, seeing she never left the chamber while Gisilhar was with the dying Herzog. But she plainly knew nothing of his alleged recantation till Hezzilo told her of it."

"What is this thou sayest?" exclaimed Hedan. "Is it possible that my mother was present when Gisilhar attended my father's deathbed?"

"She never left them together for one moment. She cannot deny it, if you ask her."

"It is well, then. Go and take my message to the Abbot. But stop! Send Pillung to me at once."

Pillung appeared presently, staggering, for he had been drinking heavily, according to his custom. The Herzog commanded him to give an exact account of the time and place when he pretended to have learnt of that secret conversation between Gisilhar and the Abbot. The churl, gathering himself up, repeated his tale.

Hedan sent him back to his work, and mounting his horse forthwith, he rode at full speed to the place where Hezzilo lived in the forest gloom. Hedan roused the priest from his hut, which, like the lair of some animal, was half underground. He requested his account of the occurrence, but it tallied exactly with Pillung's. The priest of Woden had been cunning enough to instruct his tool carefully. Hedan could not prove the lie.

As he returned, he came upon his mother who was occupied with the lading of a sumpter[23] horse. "What is the meaning of this?" asked he, with surprise.

"Didst thou not tell me the Hamelburg should be my abode? I had better go there at once."

"Thou wilt go there when I have given orders for thy going, and have provided a suitable escort," said Hedan quietly but firmly. "In two or three days I expect the workpeople here, and then I shall have to ask thee to quit the retiring chamber, but there is plenty of room beside. Choose thyself where thou wouldst be, and have thy chattels[24] taken there. Thou wilt not leave the Wirtsburg before my wedding day."

Furious at heart, but outwardly cold and quiet, she obeyed her son's behest. He was ruler indeed. Since love's tender tyranny had seized upon his heart, he had changed entirely. All his being was now bent towards the one object he desired, which, influencing his very will, had called that will into activity. He felt himself a man, and felt his power of overruling any opposition to his newly-found energy.

It had been a fatiguing day, and Hedan retired to his room to enjoy a rest on the couch of bear skins which served him for a bed at night. He did not sleep now, but soon fell into the most pleasant of day dreams, calling back to his mind the charming ride through the spring wood, and the subsequent meeting with Bellaheld. Her lovely figure, sweet and majestic, rose before him; he saw her every movement, remembered her every word, and rejoiced in the recollection. And so vivid was the morning's experience to his fancy, that he could not be surprised to hear the actual church bell calling the Hochheimer brethren to matins, as in the morning the silvery sounds stole upon his hearing, carried through the wood. But could it be? Surely not; at such a distance he must be dreaming! Yet clearer and clearer the sacred sound arose, not from Hochheim, but from the cenoby at Wirzburg, floating past him higher and higher, burdened with the thanksgiving of the whole congregation which had united at the oratory to praise the Lord for His mercy, and to ask His blessing upon the Herzog.

Yes, upon the Herzog and upon his chosen bride, for Haimerich was not the first to bring them word of the Herzog's change, one of the brethren having already sped across from Hochheim bearing the news. Haimerich's message of goodwill was therefore not unexpected. But, if he could not surprise them, he was the more surprised himself when Abbot David acquainted him with the cause of all this happiness, and great was the unlooked-for joy of the Christian people at the Burg when he returned to them with the strange account.

"To-morrow," he said, "she will receive baptism. Not at Wirzburg, but at Hochheim, where the Herzog has desired her to stay until the wedding."

Hedan remained on his couch, listening to the bell as to sweetest music. To him the sounds spoke of Bellaheld. But the charm was rudely interrupted; Geila stood before him, pale and trembling with rage. "It is only of his mother," she began, "that the new Herzog demands obedience. The strangers may laugh at his commands with impunity."

"Who laughs at my commands?" asked Hedan calmly, as he rose from his bear skins. "I permitted the Abbot to continue to worship as he was wont in my father's lifetime."

"Indeed!" said the Herzogin sharply. "Then I suppose thou spokest an untruth to insult me, when thou didst tell me this morning it was thy intention to stop the hateful thing at Hochheim also."

"That was my full intention in setting out," said Hedan. "But my mind was changed on meeting one of these objectionable people, and finding that she was actually binding up the wounds of a wretch who has tried to set fire to their very home. Then I bethought me that my father has consulted with the Folkthing[25], and that the resolution has been carried to grant the Hibernians liberty of worship; that therefore I have no right to act otherwise as it would be disregarding the desire of the Thing itself."

"Who was she that made thee think thus?" asked Geila savagely.

"Bellaheld is the maiden's name. But why shouldest thou inquire? Thou shouldest rather tell me why my father's last desire was kept from me; why I had to learn from Hezzilo and Pillung that he returned to the gods?"

"How could I tell thee," replied Geila, "seeing it was news to me when we heard it from Hezzilo?"

"News to thee? Well, then the abominable tale has to travel by crooked paths! Thou must have been the very first to know, seeing thou didst not leave him alone with Gisilhar for one moment. Yet thou didst not learn the strange story from my father—not even from Gisilhar— but only through Pillung and Hezzilo who pretended to have it from Gisilhar, though unknown to the latter. It is certainly strange."

"But I sat quite apart from thy dying father," replied Geila eagerly. "How should I have understood his whispered word? Gisilhar's ear was bent to his lips. He had come between me and my husband. And Pillung has sworn to it!"

"The six free men whom Gisilhar produced as witnesses have also sworn that my father's 'yes' to Gisilhar's question had been his last word, death overtaking him almost immediately. I mean to sift the matter. Leave me now."

The Herzogin retired, and Hedan once more sent for Pillung. "Thou hast forsworn thyself, miserable caitiff[26]!" exclaimed the young ruler, as soon as the latter appeared.

But Pillung added oath upon oath. Hezzilo had assured him he could swear falsely to any extent without fear of evil consequences if only, by way of precaution, the little finger of his left hand were pointed to the ground while the right hand was lifted in perjury. Hedan, not suspecting the sly tricks of the wicked priest, was misled by the utter confidence with which Pillung challenged the direst punishments of the gods if he spoke not the truth, and felt less sure of his doubts.

The old Herzogin, in the meantime, saw horror upon horror. That the chosen bride of her son was no other than that maiden Bellaheld, the Christian, with whom he had fallen in on his ride to Hochheim, seemed certain. Now she understood the sudden change in his bearing. It was powerful love which had made an entrance in his heart and was already beginning to rule his actions. But the thought that a daughter of these hated Hibernians should be the sharer of Hedan's throne and life was more than she could bear, for then it would be impossible to wage successful war against Christianity; to drive away these Irish messengers and pull down their cenobies. She could scarcely hope in that case to keep her son from forsaking the gods, yet this must be her one aim, the sole motive of her actions.

She took up her abode in the apartment made over to her, and far from desiring her removal to the Hamelburg, she now endeavored to secure her residence at the Wirtsburg or in its immediate neighborhood, even after the wedding.

Hedan, knowing her temper, expected she would withdraw from her seat in the hall. But when, on the following day, he obeyed the summons to dinner, he found her at her accustomed place. She rose with the respect due to the Herzog, greeting him with smiles, but made no remark as to the bride he had chosen, nor asked who she could be. Speaking, however, of the intended building operations, she expressed herself interested in all his plans. He was pleased to find she had so soon submitted to circumstances, nor saw he reason to think differently for some time.

Bellaheld had spent the rest of the day on which she had promised to be the Herzog's wife in tears and solitude, partly in the desolate cabin, partly at her mother's grave. She had yielded up to God the deep secret of her heart, a sacrifice truly, when she accepted Hedan, and now she thought not again of Gisilhar, who henceforth was dead to her. But she thought of the thorny path before her, and prayed God for strength to go along that path in obedience. Her baptism, which was now fixed for the following morning, was to her as the seal set upon this giving of her person and her life to God, accepting from Him the duty He had shaped out for her. Her clear mind had at once grasped the difficulty of her future position. She knew it would require wisdom and circumspection to meet Geila, whom she would have to honor as her husband's mother, without yielding one particle of the firmness she owed to her Christian profession. She prayed

God earnestly to give her that wisdom. She knew her weakness; it made her more humble than ever, and this feeling, together with her own desire to be a faithful handmaid of her Lord, left an impression upon her. Yet it was natural that the brethren, even the Abbot himself, should see in her the future Herzogin, and should honor her as such even now. They could do so all the more sincerely as it was not so much her future greatness, but rather the nobility of her present bearing, which they admired. They could judge of the worth of her resolve.

But poor Bellaheld could not understand why the brethren should thus honor her; it almost hurt her. She bowed her head and raised it again, as though in childlike supplication, before those who had hitherto been her spiritual fathers, and whose prayers, whose guidance, she felt she needed more than ever.

"Bellaheld," said Totman, her father's aged friend, meeting her one day, "understand me aright; it is not thy humility I would blame. Humility is as the bloom on the fruit of every Christian virtue. But I would wish thee to find thy level on this new path which the Lord has marked out for thee. Thou art to be our Herzog's wife, a princess, raised above us. Humble thyself before thy God, but do not abase thyself before us. A kindly spirit thou shouldest ever show, even to the lowest, but such kindness and inward humility need not detract from the honor due to thy position, and which should show itself in thy bearing. It is as the Herzog's wife that thou art called upon to enter the Wirtsburg, not as his inferior. His faithful wife thou shalt be; yea, more than this, the servant of thy God, and a pillar of the faith in high places. I do not say, 'Try to gain over thy husband by untimely zeal.' Thou shouldest rather bear in mind what saith St. Peter: 'Ye wives, be in subjection to your own husbands; that, if any obey not the Word, they also may without the Word be won by the conversations of the wives; while they behold your chaste conversation coupled with fear.'

"Yet there are limits beyond which even thy wifely obedience may not go. Thou must never allow thyself to be kept from prayer and from the meeting together with the brethren in the house of God, and thou must always be a faithful champion for the Christian people, man or maidservant, on the Burg. And especially will it be thy duty to hold thy own as the Herzog's wife before the old Herzogin, his mother. But how shouldest thou succeed in all this, if thou canst not learn to feel at home in thy new position even now? What if the Herzog should come to visit thee as he may any day? Dost thou think he would like thy bowing low before each one of us? It could not possibly please him. Or dost thou imagine thou couldst change thy bearing all at once?"

"Forgive me, father," said Bellaheld. "It is truly a great work I have been called to do. Its very weight has humbled me. But it is to you and the fathers I bowed. I knew I should have to walk differently as the Herzog's wife. Yet thou art right; I cannot learn new ways all at once, and must begin even now. I will try."

And she went her way, lowly at heart as ever, but showing again in her every gesture that inborn dignity and noble grace which had charmed Hedan at their meeting in the forest when he thought she must be a Valkyr maiden of Walhalla.

And who was it bursting now from the forest on a milk-white charger with the brightly polished copper shield on his left arm? It was Hedan, followed by Haimerich.

With a proud look in her eye, Bellaheld stood waiting the approach of her lord, and something like pleasure glowed on her brow. The Herzog jumped from his horse, in a transport of delight, to clasp the noble maiden who, conscious that she was his now, stood holding out her arms.

"I have come at last!" he said. "I would not come empty-handed, and the Bavarian peddler kept me waiting so long."

Haimerich, meanwhile, was undoing a package which had been fastened to the pommel of his powerful horse, and then followed the noble pair to the refectory, whither the brethren were conducting the Herzog.

"Thou art my bride," said the latter to Bellaheld. "Let me adorn thee as befitteth her whom I have chosen." And suiting the action to the word, he took from the hand of his retainer a costly robe of purple silk; also an ermine cape, bracelets, and a diadem set with precious stones. Bellaheld, at Hedan's desire, at once took these things to the nearest cabin, and looked a princess indeed when she returned, clothed in her lover's presents.

Hedan rejoiced at her beauty, and even Bellaheld had some feeling as though that future position which she had accepted with such a spirit of sacrifice, whatever of thorns it might bring, might yield its roses also. A natural delight in raiment belongs to woman. The high-minded maiden could not be accused of vanity, but, as a pledge of her lover's affection, she did value these pretty things. She felt the happiness of knowing herself loved by her future lord, and the duty of loving him in return became easier, all the more so as she found in him a man endowed with nobleness of mind and strength of character.

The company sat down to their common meal. The Abbot prayed the sixty-seventh psalm, to which the Herzog listened attentively. The board was suitably provided. The brethren and sisters, filling several long tables, contented themselves with their usual fare consisting of oatmeal porridge, vegetables, and dried fruit, but the smaller table, to which, besides Hedan and Bellaheld, only the Abbot and his wife, together with the aged Totman and honest Haimerich, were invited, showed the cenoby could offer something of cheering hospitality. There was a large pike from the Abbot's preserves, and a dish of snipe which the boy Damoalis had caught the day before. There was also wheaten cake, milk, butter and plover's eggs, and, to enhance the charms of the cake, a dish of golden honey, fresh from the comb, as well as black berries preserved in honey, to complete the feast. The Herzog having had a full morning's ride did full justice to the meal, Bellaheld and the others keeping him company, when the sound of a horse's hoofs broke in upon their ears.

"Who can it be, Haimerich?" exclaimed Hedan, but before the latter could reach the door, Pillung presented himself at the entrance with a well-conditioned roebuck on his shoulder. Catching sight of the Herzog, he showed surprise and fear.

"What is thy business here?" asked the latter.

"The Herzogin has sent me to deliver this fine roebuck, with her greeting, to the maiden Bellaheld," stammered Pillung, adding with a brazen face, "I was not told that I should meet the Herzog here."

"Rejoice, Bellaheld!" said Hedan, well pleased. "Even my mother has thought of thee with kindly feeling."

Pillung was invited to sit down with the general company. When they had risen from the table, Bellaheld showed the Herzog all over the cenoby. He admired the gardens and fish preserves, and made friends with the various members of the community. Taking his leave in the evening, he said to the Abbot, "As I am about to carry off a priceless treasure from your cenoby, it is meet that I should give you something in its stead. I herewith present you with the Foxwood and the Alder grove. Together they will be the freehold property of this cenoby for all time to come." And, handing over the title deed, he rode away, followed by the faithful Hamerich, and the less-tried Pillung.

CHAPTER 5

THE WILD HUNT

The LORD hath His way in the whirlwind and in the storm.
—Nahum 1:3

Night was falling when the Herzog, followed by his two retainers, set out on his ride. Entering the beech forest, he asked Pillung, "Whence did my mother learn who is to be the future Herzogin and where she could be found? She never inquired it of me."

Whereupon the man made answer, "How should she not know it, since the very birds are heard to sing of Bellaheld!"

Hedan could not exactly question this, but asked again, "Did she know I had gone to spend the day at Hochheim?"

"How should she, since you kept it secret, noble Herzog?"

"But she might have guessed it, seeing me deal with the peddler yesterday."

"And, moreover," added Haimerich, "I noticed her this morning watch us from behind her lattice as we rode from the Burg."

"That is not true!" returned Pillung rudely.

"I fear me thy manners have suffered," replied the Herzog good-naturedly. "Did the men of God not see to thy bodily wants?"

"More than enough, I should say," was Haimerich's opinion. "But he can never have enough, and drunkenness is not pandered to in the cenoby."

"The more fools, they!" muttered Pillung.

"What was that?" inquired the Herzog.

"I did not speak," replied the churl unmannerly.

"Thou didst, and I insist on thy repeating it," commanded Hedan.

"Well then, if you please to hear—'Poor old lady!' I said, meaning the Herzogin, your most noble mother. You may strike me; scourge me if you will, but I do pity her. She is intent only on your advantage, and you did not even do her the honor of letting her know who is to be the future Herzogin. She bears it in silence, without a word of complaint, but it cuts her to the heart. She has told me that she desires to live in peace with her daughter-in-law, and for this reason she sent her the venison as a token of goodwill. But the Herzog treats her, his own mother, as though she were a churl's wife. You mean to banish her to the Hamelburg. She will go this very night if you ask it of her, but I do know—Regiswind, her waiting woman has told me—that she spends half the nights in tears. It was only yesterday that Regiswind and myself ventured to speak words of comfort to her saying, 'Noble lady, the Herzog, your son, is a gracious master. He is now engaged in repairing the Wirtsburg. If you were to ask it of him, he would send workpeople across to Gaibach on the Hill to restore the building for your abode. You would, in that case, be near enough for any purpose. Or would you rather that we ask him for you?' But she said neither 'yes' nor 'no,' repeating merely that it was your desire that she should be banished to the Hamelburg, and she would not gainsay you."

"The Hamelburg is no banishment," said Hedan, frowning. "It is a lovely place in the heart of Thuringia!"

"Neither did she call it banishment," added Pillung hastily. "It was my foolish pity which called it so."

The Herzog rode ahead, musing. "If she wishes to dwell at Gaibach, well, I could grant her that desire. I do not want to treat her harshly; she is my mother. And she seems pleasantly inclined to the maiden I have chosen to be the Herzogin in her stead. I may as well settle her abode at Gaibach."

Haimerich, meanwhile, followed, abreast with Pillung. But the latter averted his face; he would have naught to say to a hated Christian. Whereupon Haimerich began, "I fear me, Pillung, that we shall have a heavy storm before long. The evening has been unusually sultry, and now I see clouds upon clouds rolling up ominously. This is worse than night."

Pillung made no answer, and Haimerich continued after a while, "The Lord have mercy upon us! The storm is breaking. Hark at the whistling in the treetops, and the howling in the rocky caves!"

"I hear," said Pillung carelessly. "It is Woden riding across the forest. Thou mayest well be afraid."

"I?" returned Haimerich. "No, not I. The living God is my sure defense. How should I tremble at the voice of the storm? If there were a Woden, others might have reason to fear him. Not I."

"Who art thou speaking of?" demanded Pillung savagely. "Dost thou dare to think of the Herzog?"

"I mean those," said Haimerich quietly, "who have sworn falsely, calling upon Woden to avenge it."

The Herzog, hearing this, turned in his stirrup, and saw that Pillung received this remark with a sneer. But just then Hedan's horse stumbled, requiring the full skill of his rider to rein him up and save him from coming down upon his knees. "We cannot proceed," he said. "We must abide the storm."

Darkness had closed in upon them, and the pathway, which even in broad daylight offered difficulties to the most practiced rider, was utterly impossible now. It would have been foolhardiness to attempt it. A whirlwind burst above them, covering the ground with a shower of broken branches.

"The Wild Hunt is upon us!" groaned Pillung, aghast. "We must lie with our faces to the ground, that the wrathful gods may pass over."

"Yes," said Haimerich, grimly, "and let the startled horses trample upon their cowardly riders!"

But Pillung had already suited the action to the word, and was lying flat upon the ground by the side of his horse. Had it been less dark, his companions might have seen his abject fear in his every movement; he positively shook with terror. They also had sprung from their horses, but only to hold them by the bit and speak to them reassuringly.

"Dost thou expect me to hold thy horse as well as mine?" exclaimed Haimerich.

But Pillung answered amid groans, "I must lie flat on the ground; Hezzilo said so. Then Woden cannot hurt me."

"Woden harms none who swears by him truthfully," interposed Hedan, "even though they stand on their feet. Jump up, Pillung, and attend to thy horse!"

"I cannot! I dare not!" moaned the terrified coward. "Hezzilo warned me to lie flat on the ground and let the right hand clutch the earth, calling upon Hertha's protection; then the Wild Hunt will pass over and leave me scathless. How terribly it roars!" and he groaned in anguish.

It was indeed a frightful uproar, tearing through the forest, snapping trees asunder as though they were saplings. Such was the commotion that the Herzog could scarcely hear his own voice as he made answer to Pillung, saying, "Well mayest thou fear for thy right hand! Remember how thou didst raise it in perjury at my father's funeral, saying, 'Let Woden crush it, if I have told a lie!'"

"It is safe!" cried Pillung. "He cannot hurt it!"

"But God Almighty can hurt thee," said Haimerich solemnly. And scarcely had he spoken the words when a great beech came down with a terrible crash. Hedan and Haimerich had barely time to jump aside, dragging their horses after them. They escaped safely; but not Pillung, who now lay yelling, half-buried beneath the crushing weight of the fallen tree. As they turned, a sheet of lightning for a moment lit up the scene. Pillung's horse lay crushed to death beneath the beech tree. Pillung himself appeared to have his left arm free, and was trying to extricate his right hand which had been caught by the tree. Flashes of lightning, having once begun, went on now in rapid succession, accompanied by terrific roars of thunder. The forest seemed one mass of fire.

"His arm is broken, the hand frightfully mangled!" said Haimerich, having examined the wounded man by the glare of continued flashes, the Herzog adding wrathfully, "The gods owe thee another bolt for perjuring thyself a second time when I sent for thee to my room."

"Ah, no! Spare me!" screamed the unfortunate man. "I will hide nothing. I did swear falsely, from beginning to end, as Hezzilo taught me!"

"And it is thy wickedness," said Hedan, "which has brought all this trouble upon us. Who knows but we too must perish? Call upon thy God, Haimerich. Perchance He will save us. I cannot call upon Him, and my own gods, who have just now proved their power upon Pillung, have little cause to help me, for I fear me I have done little to please them!"

"Noble Herzog," said Haimerich solemnly, "it is not the gods, but the One God, who made heaven and earth, who has thus shown His power upon this man because he perjured himself, bearing false witness against His kingdom. He is the God who hath His way in the storm, and whose fury cometh forth like fire. To Him will I call that He may keep you safe. But methinks there are others praying for you even now. Hear you not in the pauses of wind and thunder the voice of the ringing bell? Even now the men of God are on their knees in the oratory, and Bellaheld among them, calling upon God to hold you safe."

Yes, Hedan heard it ever and anon amid the rolling thunder, sweet and pure as on that Easter morn. Poor little bell; what availeth thy trustful voice against the raging commotion? Even now, the forking fire shot from the heavens, yet strangely, the hungry flashes touched not the spot where

Haimerich knelt in prayer by the side of his Herzog, where Pillung lay chained in agony. Rivers of rain presently flooded the ground, and the bursts of thunder came at greater intervals. But amid the rustling rain floated the silvery sounds speaking of Bellaheld to Hedan's ear, and away into the valley rolled the voice of thunder. The little bell had had the victory. Hedan stood touched to the heart.

But the bell also died away into silence. Rain continued, and the enclosing darkness left not the faintest chance of light.

"How shall we succeed in freeing the wretched man from his position?" asked Haimerich.

"And how shall we succeed in finding a way home?" returned the Herzog by way of answer, at the same time trying to peer into the hopeless night.

It was vain. They could not even guess at the direction where a path might lie, and, had they seen, they would probably have found it barred by fallen trees. It was a most helpless situation. But what is this—a nearing radiance in the far depth of the night, now brighter, now gliding among the shadows? White garments, lit up by torches, presently appeared amid the trees, now hidden for a moment, now more vivid, gaining upon the distance.

"It is Colman the Abbot, with some of the brethren!" exclaimed Haimerich, after a moment of surprise. "They have come to bring you help."

When Colman and his companions reached the place and found that both the Herzog and Haimerich had escaped the storm unhurt, they broke into loud acclamations of praise and thanksgiving.

"But what has become of Pillung?" they asked.

"There he is, all but dead for his perjury," replied Hedan.

The brethren at once turned to the unfortunate man, setting themselves to free him from his painful position. Pillung had lost consciousness, but the touch to his fractured limb was enough to revive him.

He started with a scream of agony. As soon as this had subsided, the Herzog, bending over him, said sternly, "Tell me, is it true, that story of thine, of a conversation with my mother? If it is true, then swear to it."

"Swear? No, no, I cannot swear!" cried Pillung, full of horror.

"Then tell me the simple truth. All this tale of pity for her and that proposal of Gaibach as her residence is merely thy repeating what she herself has told thee?"

"It is, it is! You know everything, most dread Herzog! You see in darkness, as though you had Woden's eyes!" cried Pillung, adding after a while, "And she sent the roebuck to deceive the low-born wench and her lover, she said. I could swear to it."

"Well, I believe thee without an oath," said Hedan. "As for the lies thou hast told me before, I might well have the tongue plucked from thy head. But thou hast ample punishment for all thy misdeeds."

And, addressing himself to the rest of the party, he continued, "What advice have the brethren to give me? We must be halfway between the Wirtsburg and Hochheim. Whither had we best direct our steps?"

"We will escort you to your own Burg," said the Abbot. "We can spend the rest of the night with our brethren there and return to Hochheim to-morrow."

"I would gladly accept this proposal, were it not for Bellaheld, who ought to know we are safe," objected the Herzog.

"Then two of the brethren shall return at once," decided

Colman. "The rest of us can show you the way."

The two having been dispatched, two others tried to make Pillung walk between them, but Haimerich would not hear of this. "He is too weak," he said. "Lift him to my horse, Brother Waldo, and mount behind him to support his arm. I will take the lead with a torch."

Slowly and cautiously the little company moved though the wood, picking their way amid the ruins of the storm. It was long past midnight when they reached the foot of the Wirtsburg. Pillung was given over to the charge of the cenoby; his arm had to be amputated.

On the following morning, Hezzilo also lost his right hand by the Herzog's command, and Geila was banished to the Hamelburg.

CHAPTER 6

ILL WEEDS GROW APACE

That which is born of the flesh is flesh. —John 3:6

The day had come on which Hedan brought home his bride. According to the old Thuringian custom, it was on a Tuesday. The Herzog had invited the nobles from the country round about to be present at the wedding; they and their retainers accompanied him to Hochheim in grand procession. Some of his guests were

Christians, others more or less well-inclined to Christianity, while most were anxious to uphold the worship of the gods. As far as the wedding was concerned, this offered no difficulty. In the early time of the Christian religion, marriage was a purely civil act, in which the Church had no part, beyond the congregation's prayer for a blessing on the couple, spoken on the Sunday following the ceremony. By degrees, however, the custom obtained, that a Christian couple stated their desire to marry one another in the presence of a presbyter, who, having witnessed to this, added his blessing.

Hedan and Bellaheld, having already expressed such a desire on their part in the hearing and knowledge of Abbot Colman, had no need of doing so a second time. When the Herzog arrived at Hochheim to fetch his bride, he was met by Colman and Totman at the entrance of the oratory, where the united congregation had prayed for a blessing on the noble pair. Totman, having been the oldest friend of Bellaheld's father, led the maiden to her husband. Before quitting his hand, Bellaheld sank to her knees, asking the old man's blessing. Hedan would have done likewise, but felt reproved by the frowns of his heathen companions. Totman, nevertheless, whose right hand was laid on Bellaheld's head as she knelt before him in her bridal wreath, included the Herzog in the blessing, praying God to grant him wisdom in ruling, and strength at all times to confess and stand by the truth as far as might be given to him to see it. "May she be a true and faithful wife to you," he added. "The Lord hath brought you together, and what God hath joined together, let not man put asunder."

The Herzog had come with rich presents to the cenoby. Droves of cows and sheep had followed the procession and were now made over to the community. But the brethren and sisters also had taken care that the bride should not go empty-handed to her husband's house. A wagon stood in readiness, drawn by bullocks decked with garlands. The wagon was to convey Bellaheld's humble dowry, left her by her mother and added to by the community, according to their power. There was a goodly store of homespun wool and linen, a spindle and distaff wreathed with flowers, a bedstead of maplewood and furnished with bear and roe skins. But the greatest treasure which the men of God could send with the bride to her new home, was that Gospel book of which Gertrude had read to Bellaheld's dying mother.

A bridal feast had been laid in the refectory, for which the Herzog himself had provided the choicest venison. When the meal had been partaken of, the Christian maidens accompanied their sister Bellaheld as far as the ring-fence which enclosed the cenoby. She took leave of them tenderly, bidding a wistful goodbye to Totman and the true-hearted Gertrude, and having mounted the palfrey[27] provided for her, the young Herzogin rode away by the side of her husband, followed by his noble retinue.

The path leading through the forest had been cleared by Hedan's orders. Near the rock where he had first seen Bellaheld, the boy Damoalis and Kathalt, who had recovered from his wounds, stopped their passage, holding a rope between them as they stood, one on each side of the path. The Herzog laughed, throwing a coin to each. Damoalis and Kathalt caught his gift with a merry shout and allowed them to pass.

Kathalt's hatred of Christianity had vanished under the loving treatment he had received at the hands of the brethren. He was being instructed in the truth, and he loved the boy Damoalis, to whom, in a measure, he owed his life.

When the bridal procession came forth from the beech

wood, the bell at Wirzburg proclaimed the joyful event. Abbot David and his brethren stood waiting their approach by the river and sang the forty-fifth Psalm while the bridal party, with horses and wagons, were ferried across. When they had landed, the Abbot stepped up to the noble pair, offering them his greeting. "The Lord shall preserve your going out and your coming in from this time forth, and even for evermore."

Hedan thanked him, waving his hand, but rode on at once. Halfway up the mount, where the approach to the Burg was guarded by outworks, the Herzog's retainers awaited their master. They also stopped the passage by holding a rope across the path. When Hedan had paid the expected toll, the heathen company struck up the usual wedding song, which the Christian bride could not listen to without a blush. She closed her eyes and could have wished to close her ears as well.

But, painful as this incident was to her feelings of modesty, she soon forgot it in the more painful expectation of meeting the old Herzogin. As the company entered the inner court, she looked anxiously about her, fearful of seeing the fanatical heathen in whose alleged kindly disposition towards her she reposed but little faith.

Hedan noticed her inquiring gaze, and said quickly, "My mother has retired to her widow's abode at the Hamelburg."

Bellaheld turned to her husband with grateful eyes. His words had removed a heavy weight from her heart. But great was the surprise with which she now looked about her—the Burg seemed a marvel of repairs. It was higher than before, for the old shingle roof had been replaced by an elevation covered with chalkstone. In fact, it now was a splendid edifice to her inexperienced eyes. Her astonishment could but be added to as she entered the hall. How high and airy! The walls and ceiling were whitewashed and decked with garlands of oak leaves! The hall, formerly so dark and dingy, was positively bright and cheerful.

The Herzog had succeeded in all his endeavors, even to the windows. From the far-off town of Lutetia[28], in the country of the Westrasian Franks, he had procured small plates of pellucid feldspar[29], which, fixed in lead after the fashion still seen in old church windows, admitted the daylight very fairly, and, though somewhat yellow of appearance, were certainly an improvement upon the mere lattice.

In the upper part of the hall, dinner was laid for the Herzog and his newly-married wife; three successive tables below being prepared for his guests, his retainers, and the servants of the Burg. The former, according to old habit, on laying aside their swords, would have thrust them crosswise into the floor, but the bare earth now was covered with flags. With evident annoyance, they returned the swords to their sheaths.

"Things have changed now from what we and our fathers have been accustomed to," said Thiotbert, one of the heathen guests, loud enough for Hedan to hear, "but, by Tuesco, surely we are not denied the bridal march!"

"No," returned Hedan, "you shall have your desire." And, taking his hat, he tossed it toward the dais, whispering to Bellaheld, "Throw thy shoe after it."

Bellaheld hesitated a moment, not knowing the dance and its preliminaries, or whether she as a Christian ought to join. She looked imploringly at her husband and, in doing so, accidentally caught the eye of Haimerich, who stood behind him and gave her a quick nod of encouragement. Thereupon she took her right shoe and flung it after her husband's hat.

But Hedan had seen the glance, and said with evident displeasure, "Thou hast no need to consult my retainer. I ask nothing that goes against thy faith." And, taking her by the hand, he opened the dance, the guests by pairs joining in procession to the anything-but-melodious sounds of a buffalo horn.

"It was not to Haimerich I looked for an answer," now whispered Bellaheld, "but to you, my husband. It was mere accident that my eye caught his."

"I rejoice to hear it," said Hedan. "Thou art never to forget that I am to be nearest and dearest, and thou must look to me in everything. Have I not parted with my own mother, lest she should come between thee and me?"

Bellaheld pressed his hand gratefully. The slight shadow of misunderstanding had vanished, the wedding feast ran its happy course, and Bellaheld watched the merry dancing of the humbler portion of her husband's household, which terminated the festivity.

Happy weeks followed. Bellaheld's new life was not so full of thorns as she had anticipated. Hedan loved her passionately, and did what he could to please her. He never interfered in any way with the practice of her religion; he even began by accompanying her every Sunday as far as the cenoby. But he never entered, and she wisely forbore pressing him to join in the worship. Nor did she know that the real reason of his going with her was a feeling of jealousy, lest she should have an opportunity of entering into conversation with his Christian retainer, Haimerich. But, judging presently that his jealousy was altogether unwarranted, he gave up accompanying her, and she walked to the cenoby with those of the women servants who were Christians.

She showed unvarying kindness to all her servants,

Christian or heathen alike, and practiced great forbearance with the ill habits of the latter. Her daily duties were much the same as would be expected now-a-days of a well-to-do farmer's wife. She had been carefully trained in the cenoby, and she set about governing her women with great tact and firmness. But every morning, before entering upon the day's labor, she gathered the Christian women-servants about her, to read with them a portion of the Gospel, and to offer up prayer. The Christian retainers and men-servants soon listened to this daily worship, gathering one-by-one at her window. When she noticed their attendance, she begged her husband to allow them a place of meeting where they might unite in prayer amongst themselves. Hedan gave the solicited permission.

One day, a heathen maidservant, to whom the young mistress had shown loving care in illness, expressed her desire to listen to the reading in the morning. Bellaheld, of course, gave her joyful leave.

The Herzogin also did not forget to visit the poor and sick about her, making no distinction of religion, if any needed her aid. She never pressed Christianity upon the heathen that thus came under her influence, but neither did she forego any opportunity of showing that her religion was the living source of the self-forgetting charity which she practiced among them. And, whenever she discovered that a case of illness was being treated with heathen sorcery, she insisted on the latter being given up if she should continue with her remedies and her prayerful attendance. And she soon found, to her great delight, that her heathen neighbors valued her kindness and rested greater confidence in her means than in the charms and jugglery of the artful priests. Some of those she thus came into contact with even begged her to give them Christian instruction, but she always referred them to the cenoby.

Thus her Christian influence spread about her, quietly but surely. One only seemed altogether untouched by it, and that was he who witnessed most of Bellaheld's purity, gentleness, patience, and loving obedience. Hedan kept his word as a man of honor, granting protection and full liberty to all Christian people about him, and showing kindness to both cenobies, more especially to that at Hochheim, but it never entered his mind to assist at any opportunity of Christian worship. He fully approved of his wife's ways and doings; he was even proud to hear her spoken of everywhere with love and veneration, but he never entered into conversation with her concerning the respective merits of her religion or his.

Some months had passed when Pillung, having recovered from his accident, returned to the Burg. Hedan could not fail to notice a marked change in his life. He never saw him intoxicated; never heard him swear. His very countenance seemed clothed in truth and honesty, instead of the slyness of expression which had formerly disgraced it. But, seeing him join the Christian men at morning prayers, the Herzog asked, astonished, whether he too had forsaken the gods.

Pillung answered, "I have learnt to serve the true God who found me in the forest and brought to light my falsehood. Ah, noble Herzog, you also were a witness to His finding me and giving me the wages of my sin. Will you not acknowledge Him to be God?"

"I have not asked you to preach to me," said Hedan, turning his back upon him.

Nor was it altogether surprising. Hedan loved not Bellaheld for the sake of her faith, but he showed kindness to those who were of her faith, instead of hating them as before, for the sake of Bellaheld, whom he loved passionately. It is true he could not forget that this love had come to him on seeing the maiden show kindness to an enemy, when he felt the breath and the beauty of another Spirit than the gods he knew. But that grace of heaven-born charity, which is more than mere earthly love of man and woman, was to him only an additional charm enhancing the sweet picture which had so suddenly filled his soul.

For Bellaheld's sake he could put up with that God who was near to her, present with her—her God, but not his! It was enough for him if, through her, he enjoyed the protection of that God; if in answer to her prayers he partook of His favor. It was enough for him, he thought. That his wife's God must become his God was an uncomfortable idea, for he felt that he too, in that case, would have to change much in his life; that he would be obliged to yield up his own will in many things, and accept the teaching and admonition of the men of God, and that was more than his pride could brook.

Neither did he consider conversion to Christianity a wise proceeding in the light of worldly wisdom. Most of the high-born in Thuringia and beyond it were still in the bonds of heathenism; so much so that, when his father was prevailed upon to accept baptism, many of his noble followers threatened to leave him and join the Saxons. It seemed, therefore, politic to keep to the former state of things, as far as he was concerned. Let the men of God first succeed in Christianizing the land, then he too might consider the advisability of becoming a Christian.

Pillung having lost his right hand, and consequently becoming unfit for labor in the ordinary sense, was now generally employed in running errands. One day he was dispatched to the Hamelburg with a letter for the old Herzogin. But, so much afraid was he of meeting her, that, when she admitted him to her presence in order to give him her answer, his looks showed so little of that peace and honesty of countenance now general with him, that Geila, knowing nothing of his conversion, saw no change in him beyond his being maimed.

"Ha!" she cried, "I fear me, both Pillung and Hezzilo had to pay dearly for a false oath! Woden took thy right hand, and my son took Hezzilo's. But why dost thou quake in thy shoes? I do not blame thee, and I am sorry for thy mishap. And I pity thee for having to live in a house where the gods are treated lightly."

"Lady,—" said Pillung, but she cut him short, continuing, "And what about my precious daughter-in-law? I hear the people think much of her. She has turned their heads as she turned my son's with her arts. But there will be an end of this soon. I may as well tell thee, for thou knowest how to be silent. The heathen nobles throughout the land will no longer put up with the Hibernian strangers. They are going to give the Herzog his choice: either to send away the low-born minx he has made his wife, and drive all these Christians from the land, or else they will turn from him and join the Saxons, and he will rue it! Do not interrupt me—I tell thee, before ye are many months older, banished Geila will have had her revenge. Now get thee back with this letter to my son."

She turned from him abruptly, leaving Pillung altogether startled by the revelation she so imprudently had made to him. But no sooner had he recovered himself than he sped on his way, running day and night to acquaint the Herzog with the news.

Hedan was greatly enraged in learning of the treacherous

intentions of the nobles in question. But, instead of being led to embrace Christianity, and to act openly and boldly towards his adversaries, he hoped to gain over his faithless followers by cowardly concession and unjust treatment of his most faithful friends. He wrote letters of appeal to the heathen nobles, denouncing any suspicion that he could enter the service of the strange God, calling to witness the fact, which was true enough, that he had never once been seen to enter the oratory. If his wife was a Christian, well, that was his business. He had found her in everything else his true and faithful wife, and if he allowed the Hibernians in general to serve their God in peace, it was no more than the Folkthing had agreed to in his father's lifetime. Thus he wrote to the disaffected nobles. But, to his mother he sent an invitation to take up her residence at Gaibach, thus apparently meeting her cherished desire, while in reality he was anxious to have her near enough to watch her. That she, too, in her turn now could watch him, he considered not.

Haimerich very foolishly expressed his disapprobation of this step, as he was out hunting with his master.

"I am grieved you should have thought so little what the Herzogin may have to bear in allowing your mother to return to this neighborhood."

"Did my wife charge thee with a message to me?" retorted Hedan, nettled, barely listening to his retainer's assertations that she had never breathed a word to him, either concerning this trouble or aught else. The result was that the very next day Geila was invited to the Wirtsburg.

It was the first time that the two women met. Bellaheld had prepared herself to accept with patience whatever of spite or hatred Geila might show her, but the artful woman went up to her with the most fawning deference, flattering her after a manner which could only rouse Bellaheld's horror of falsehood, and interspersing all this with constant hints of the respect due to the wife of the Herzog. The noble truthfulness of Bellaheld could not accept so false a means of intercourse. She retired within herself. She was silent, appearing cold and proud—the very result Geila had hoped for. Hedan noticed his wife's reserve, and resented it. Geila presently mentioned her own father, and that he had been a Herzog in Saxon lands. Bellaheld could have answered that her father, too, had come of noble, even royal stock, but she spurned the satisfaction of vain boasting, and bore the imputation that accounted her as of mean birth.

Geila spent the night at the Wirtsburg, to return on the following morning to Gaibach. That evening, Hedan informed the Herzogin that morning prayers must be stopped on that day, as it would be a great offense in the sight of his mother.

As for Geila, he watched her closely, and indeed he had plenty of reason for mistrusting her. But, his very fear of her intrigues made him anxious to consult her desires. He hoped to disarm her by speaking to her mind. "It is strange," he said, "that the gods should have punished that deceit which Hezzilo meant to practice in their honor. There is Pillung, who took Woden to witness of his false oath, and behold, Woden crushes his right hand. How should one doubt the power of the gods?"

That Pillung himself had come to disbelieve it entirely by accepting Christianity, he did not tell his mother. He had, moreover, considered it prudent to dispatch Pillung on a several days' errand before inviting Geila. But, more than this, he stopped morning prayers once and for all. Those who cared to pray might do so by themselves, he said.

Bellaheld obeyed. The thorny path was opening before her. She saw Hedan's affection for her cooled visibly. Whole days he would now spend away from her out hunting, or shut up in his old apartment where he dispatched whatever business of administration or jurisdiction required his attention. During the first months of their wedded life, he had never failed to consult her, glad that she should share his thoughts and occupations. Now, coldness and reserve had taken the place of open trust, and he all but repented of having married a Christian wife. Love seemed buried and gone.

Cause for annoyance, no doubt, was amply at hand. His hopes of conciliating the disaffected nobles by turning against his Christian friends had failed, and before long he was surprised with the unpleasant news that Horsa, the Herzog of the Saxons, had invaded the land, and that numbers of the heathen nobles had joined him.

Messengers were dispatched in all directions. The people were called to arms. Preparation for war was the one topic of the day.

"In another week, we shall be ready to take the field," said Hedan one evening, having inspected the warriors that had gathered round him.

When he retired for the night, he found Bellaheld in tears. "What is the matter?" he inquired.

"How should I not weep," replied she, "when I see you depart for cruel war? Shall you return? My heart is full of fear."

"Thou wast different when I first knew thee," returned he impatiently. "A brave maiden, I thought. I hate a whining woman. I had rather have thee pray for me as thou didst on that night when the Wild Hunt was upon us in the forest."

"Do you think, my husband, that these tears prevent my

prayers? Yes, truly will I pray for you, day and night without ceasing. Yet it is not the same thing whether prayer be offered in happy trust or with a heavy heart."

"I do not understand thee."

"Bear with me, my husband! The Christian's prayer is not like a charm by which God in heaven could be forced to do our will. He is the Lord Almighty, holy and just. What availeth all my prayer if He will not hear? And can He hear it, bless and protect one who, having had such powerful evidence of His nearness and saving mercy, has never yet owned Him to be God, nor desired to be taught His law?"

"I have kept my word," said he gruffly. "I never interfered with the cenoby. I have done my duty."

"To us, yes, but not to yourself for your own salvation. Whose protection will you rest in? The true God of the Christians you will not serve, and the heathen gods you no longer believe in."

"Who told thee I believe not in our gods? Leave me alone with thy preaching!" and he turned from her.

Before Hedan took the field, he had a meeting with the Bavarian Herzog, Theudo. It was important for him to renew alliance with this powerful ruler who could act as a strong bulwark in the South should the Chawari avail themselves of his absence and repeat their attack. As Theudo was a Christian, Hedan hoped to gain him the more easily if Bellaheld, his Christian wife, accompanied him. The meeting was to take place halfway between Wirzburg and Reginsburg.

Hedan arrived with his wife and a numerous retinue, to make up which, his Christian subjects had been chosen by preference. The homesteads of two freemen were the appointed quarters; one for the Bavarians, the other for the Thuringians, the free space in the middle being the neutral meeting ground. The two rulers, with their retinue, entered almost simultaneously at opposite sides. Bellaheld was at her place close by Hedan, but no sooner had she raised her eye than she grew pale and trembled.

It was but a moment before she recovered herself, but her emotion had not escaped the Herzog. He looked about to discover the possible cause. Among all those they had come to meet, there was but one whose unexpected appearance could trouble Bellaheld, being the only one who was no stranger at Wirzburg—Gisilhar of the Arch.

Poor Bellaheld had indeed been fearful lest Gisilhar should be of Herzog Theudo's company. How gladly would she have withdrawn her own presence, but she could not; dared not! How could she have told her husband, prone to jealousy as he was, that she had met this Gisilhar once before, and that, for one short hour, his memory had lived in her heart? Had she not sacrificed whatever of tenderness she had felt for him on the altar of her wedded troth, transferring all love to the husband that had been given to her? And, if she trembled now, it was not that she had hoped to meet Gisilhar again, but because she had feared doing so.

Transactions began, soon engaging the young Herzogin upon more pressing realities, and, in a measure, calming her fears. A treaty was arrived at, but Theudo, in agreeing to it, had stipulated that, during Hedan's absence, the cenobies and the men of God, as well as their worship, should not in any way be interfered with, and that, in case of interference by any one, they should always have free appeal to Theudo himself, as guarantee of their liberties. Hedan very naturally raised objection upon objection to this point. At this point, however, with a courage and decision he had not looked for in his wife, Bellaheld said, "I consider this clause of vital importance. Without it, my husband's mother will leave no stone unturned in her endeavors to destroy the Christian faith."

The time had come when Bellaheld, the Herzogin, remembering the duty pointed out to her by the aged Totman, must stand by her Christian subjects, even to the claiming of her right as the Herzog's wife, against Geila, his mother.

She saw it was her divinely appointed position to become a bulwark of the faith in high places, as Totman had said. She would not fail in her calling. Had she not brought her very heart to the sacrifice, even to the yielding up of life's happiness? And should she now not grasp the object of that sacrifice, in spite of the look of hot displeasure darted at her by her husband?

Business over, he returned with her to their quarters. His first words on being alone with her was the question, "Where didst thou meet Gisilhar before?"

She returned his burning gaze calmly, and said, "It was he who brought me from Wirzburg to Hochheim on Easter morn when I was called to my mother's dying bed."

"If that is all, why didst thou start at his sight?"

"I was fearful lest I should meet him again, and it troubled me."

Hedan paced the floor in silence, wondering whether it could be merely the recollection of the mournful occasion of their first meeting which made the second undesirable, but, far from feeling satisfied, he asked presently, placing himself face-to-face with his wife, "Did he woo thee, when you met before?"

"In sooth, the time would have been ill-chosen," she replied, adding after a while, "It is not fair in my husband to question or doubt me. Is it not enough that I have come to you a pure-handed maiden? If you had required a wife which had never looked upon a man before, you might be prepared for disappointment!" And she turned from him indignant and hurt, trying to hide her tears.

At this moment Haimerich entered, announcing dinner. Herzog Theudo awaited their company. Hedan could not delay. Bellaheld begged to be excused, but Hedan would not hear of it, saying that she must, in any case, appear at his side, whereupon she dried her tears and went.

Gisilhar, being a free lord, had his place at Theudo's own table, and Bellaheld found him sitting opposite to her. "I little thought," he began, as soon as he had the opportunity, "that I should meet you again as Herzogin. This was hardly to be foreseen when I accompanied you to Hochheim on Easter Day. Indeed, other thoughts seemed nearer then, and who knows—had your mother not been dying, who knows but that another might have stepped in between you and your present honors!"

"Indeed!" returned Bellaheld, coldly. "Methinks I should have been the first to consult; not you, nor another! And it seems to me your conversation is ill-befitting a Christian man, as I take you to be." And she dropped her eyes with marked displeasure, allowing him not another word.

But he had noticed she had been crying, and from all he had seen and heard besides, he had gathered a tolerably correct estimate of her position.

"She is made unhappy," he said to himself, "not only by her fanatical mother-in-law, but also by the jealous temper of her husband. She married him, hoping to further the interests of Christianity, and now she feels it a sacrifice beyond endurance. But why has he married her? For some sudden love which did not last? It is plain she is no happy wife. I must watch her."

But Hedan, too, was drawing conclusions. "How brazen-faced of the man, to own in my very hearing that he entertained thoughts of her, and who knows but he does so still! And how anxious she was to silence him, lest I should hear more! It is plain to me they love one another. A fool I am to believe her true to me! And, I bethink me, did she not swoon in very anguish when I first asked her to be my wife? But I shall know how to keep them apart."

The following morning, the party returned to the Wirtsburg. No sooner had they arrived there than Hedan sent for his mother, requesting her to take her abode at the Burg during his absence in order to keep careful watch upon Bellaheld, lest at any time she should meet with Gisilhar who, he doubted not, would soon put in an appearance.

"Now I understand," he said, "why she was so anxious to place the Thuringian Christians under Herzog Theudo's protection. She hoped it might open a way for her old lover to come and go at his pleasure."

He then demanded Bellaheld's faithful promise that under no pretence whatever would she leave the Burg until he returned. "I shall go every Sunday to the cenoby," said she, "and I shall read and pray every morning with the Christian servants here. I claim the right of your given promise."

The Herzog was furious, but Bellaheld remained firm, though otherwise patient as a lamb, and not answering a word to the wicked hints of the evil-minded Geila. Hedan saw he could not prevail.

"Then give me your word at least," he cried, "that you will not go further than the cenoby while I am away."

"This I will promise," she said. "I am well content with

the liberty of joining the worship in the oratory, and ask no more."

This settled, the Herzog sent a messenger to the cenoby, requiring the Abbot's oath that no visitor should be admitted during his absence.

"This is interfering with our lawful rights," said Abbot David, and went to speak to the Herzog himself. Arrived at the Burg, he met numbers of Christian nobles who had joined Hedan's cause. These, upon hearing the Abbot's grievance, went in with him to the Herzog, saying, "Unless you give your word to the Abbot that both cenobies shall continue in full liberty even now in your absence, you may go to war without us."

"Is it not foolish, O Herzog," said Ruodbert, their spokesman, "to alienate your Christian friends? It is the heathen nobles who have turned against you. We Christians are true to our allegiance. Why should you thus grieve us?"

Hedan saw that he was helpless unless he agreed to their demands, and gave the required oath. Geila, too, was forced to swear she would keep the peace.

At night, Hedan retired to his solitary chamber and, when Bellaheld woke in the morning, her women told her that the Herzog, with all his host, had departed.

CHAPTER 7

PATIENT IN TRIBULATION

I know how to be abased. —Philippians 4:12

Shortly after Hedan's departure, Geila took up her residence at the Wirtsburg. She was followed by her attendants; men and women, all of whom, of course, were heathen. But more than this, a number of heathen priests returned with her, bringing up wagons containing all the utensils considered needful for pagan sacrifice. Within a few days, the whole aspect of the Burg was changed. Bellaheld, her women, and a few aged retainers were the only Christians left. These were rudely pushed aside while the heathen, priests and all, ruled the place. Geila at once took it upon herself to play the mistress, Bellaheld submitting in silence. But her worst time was at meals, when Geila taunted her with all manner of insult in the hearing of the assembled household.

"Thou wilt soon return to whence thou camest," she said. "When my son comes back, he will separate from the low-born creature who is no better than a beggar. Thou shalt have leave then to join thy lover Gisilhar, for aught we care."

"I have no lover save the Herzog," said Bellaheld proudly, "and if you care to know my descent, I am as nobly born, perchance, as my husband. My father's uncle was King of Dundalk."

Geila burst into a mocking laughter. "Dundalk!" she cried, "and where may this kingdom be? As large as our dairy farm, I warrant me!"

"He was a free lord of his clan. Such are called kings with us."

"I perceive," sneered Geila, "that is why the free lord Gisilhar could so easily become king of thy heart. Birds of a feather—I see! But, when the Herzog returns, you shall be put to the fire ordeal. If thou art as pure as thou wouldst have us believe, thy feet can walk upon the burning embers scathless."

To such language she treated her day after day. Poor Bellaheld was scarcely able to eat for sorrow and grief. Her health began to suffer and she saw that she and her hopes would perish if this continued. She consequently refused to appear in the hall, and retired to one of the spare chambers, where at least she could have peace, requesting to have her meals served there. Geila sent her the remains of the servants' table, but Bellaheld was satisfied.

In the morning, she continued to gather the few Christian people about her to read the Gospel with them and unite in prayer, which alone could uphold them in trouble. However, the little congregation was often obliged to take refuge in a small garret room behind her chamber in order to get away from the yelling which the heathen servants made a point of striking up before Bellaheld's window whenever they thought her engaged in worship. The wild singing of coarse songs, in honor of the heathen gods, in itself was a trouble to be borne, and whenever the Christian servants ventured abroad, they were reviled and buffeted. They could but remember what their Lord had said, "Behold, I send you forth as sheep among wolves."

It was on the second Sunday after Hedan's departure that Bellaheld, at the head of her little flock, left the Burg amid the scornful laughter of her adversaries. She was on her way to the cenoby some time before the bell began to call to worship, and thereby gained her object: to secure half an hour in which she might unbosom herself to the faithful Abbot, telling him of her grief and receiving his advice and consolation. She found him alone in his cabin, and was in the midst of her tale of sorrow when the door of the adjoining room was flung open and Gisilhar burst in who, having heard of her trouble, could no longer restrain himself.

"For heaven's sake!" she exclaimed, terrified. "How is it that you are here?"

"I have come on Theudo's business," replied he. "I arrived last night, intending to watch from here how Geila fulfils her oath. This is the way, then, in which the woman keeps her promise? Very well. I am here now, and I will teach her better."

"For God's sake, do not interfere!" cried Bellaheld, "unless you mean to ruin me entirely. She has not yet troubled our worship here, and her treatment of myself is of no consequence to you."

"Bellaheld!" said Gisilhar tenderly, "there was a time when thou didst not use the 'you' in addressing me. Canst thou not trust me as thou didst then? Thou hast joined thyself in wedlock to this heathen, meaning to do well, but the great sacrifice thou hast brought for the Christian cause has availed thee nothing. It grieves me beyond measure to see thee suffer. Ah, Bellaheld, I have not changed since then. Indeed I honor and love thee all the more. This union with a heathen is no marriage; it cannot be binding. By the word of the Apostle, thou art free to depart from him who first departed from thee, giving thee over to thine enemy. St. Paul says, 'For what knowest thou, O wife, whether thou shalt save thy husband?' and also, 'A brother or a sister is not under bondage in such cases.' Come with me. I will take thee in safety to Herzog Theudo's court, and he himself will pronounce thy divorce."

"That I might be free to marry you?" said Bellaheld scornfully. "Truly a tempting offer, but I say to you, 'Get thee behind me. Thou art an offence unto me!' I have taken my oath not to leave the Wirtsburg while my husband is absent in the war. But, quite apart from this, it needed not an oath to make me choose the path of duty. It is not true that Hedan departed from me in the sense you would have it, and the Apostle says, 'The woman which hath an husband that believeth not, and if he be pleased to dwell with her, let her not leave him.' I am his true wife, and I will keep him the faith I have pledged him before God. Tempt me not to dishonor the name of Christ, be false to His people, and lay them open to the Herzog's vengeance."

"The men of God are under the special protection of Herzog Theudo," said Gisilhar, "and he can keep them safe better than thou couldst. And they are further protected by Childebert, the powerful king of the Franks who has united under scepter Neustria, Burgundy, and Austrasia, and who will no longer allow these Thuringian Herzogs to play the part of independent rulers, considering they have been obliged to acknowledge the supremacy of the Frankish kings for nearly two centuries now. No, Bellaheld, it needs not thy sacrifice to keep the men of God safe. Why shouldest thou suffer these things?"

"I have but one answer," said Bellaheld. "Nothing will happen to me but what is the will of God. Yet one word to you, Gisilhar. You say you love me—I crave not your love, but I may well ask for Christian charity. It was your foolish, unguarded behavior the other day which caused my husband to put me in the charge of the cruel Geila, lest I should meet you in his absence. If you will add to my sorrows, you have but to remain here. But if you have a kindly feeling for me, I pray you, leave the country before Geila becomes aware of your presence, or, if this is against Herzog Theudo's command, at least take your abode at Hochheim, and not at Wirzburg."

"Yes," interposed the Abbot now, "let this be your decision. It is enough. The bell is ringing, and I must enter the oratory. Thou, Gisilhar, shalt remain in my cabin, and I forbid thee to show thyself to anyone. I myself will take care to see thee to Hochheim in the night."

Gisilhar, having both the Abbot and the Herzogin against him, retired as he was bid. Bellaheld accompanied the Abbot to the oratory, and, after hearing the Word and partaking of the Lord's Supper, refreshed and strengthened in spirit, she left the cenoby with her companions to enter, with a willing heart, upon another week of sorrow.

But, arriving at the Burg, she found the household gathered in the court, evidently intent upon what news they could gather from one in their midst. Bellaheld went nearer, if possible, to hear what he had to say, when, to her intense delight, she saw it was Pillung himself—Pillung, who had set out with the expedition, and who had now returned, dispatched by the Herzog after battle.

"Pillung!" she cried. "What of my husband?"

"Ha, the Herzogin, herself!" exclaimed the messenger. "To you I am sent with news of a great victory, which the Herzog, with his Christian followers, has won over the rebel heathen. But enter your own hall, noble lady. It is to you, in the place of honor, that I will deliver my message. If others like to listen, they may hear that none of the heathen rebels escaped."

Geila retired to her room, but Bellaheld once more sat in her rightful place in the hall, the people gathering about her, while Pillung, mounting a stool, delivered himself of his report.

"The Herzog had safely crossed the Rhon and was passing through the valley of the Wesra when his scouts returned with the information that the whole array of the enemy—the Saxons together with the disaffected Thuringians—had been seen on the banks of the Horsila, beyond the forest. The Herzog then took counsel with his faithful nobles. Some were for climbing the mountain called the 'High Suona,' from the fact that justice there is delivered to the people, and, from that height, to make a descent upon the enemy. Others, again, were afraid of an open battle because the enemy was far stronger than we. They were rather for enticing him into ravines and hollows, where numbers would not avail.

"The Herzog took position upon the Suona with his vanguard. Then Haimerich spoke to me, saying, 'Pillung, wouldst thou do good service to the Christian cause?' 'Yes,' said I, 'even if it should cost me my life.' 'Then exchange thy warrior's coat for a peddler's jerkin[30]' he said. 'Let me batter thee about a little, that thou mayest have a few scratches to show. Go down into the valley of the Horsila and get thee to the camp of the rebel Thuringians. Tell them that Hedan and his vanguard are on the top of the Suona, and that one of his men had thus beaten thee. They will ask thee about his force, and thou shalt say truthfully that the body of his fighting men are still behind; that he alone with twenty nobles and their followers had climbed the mountain.'

"I did as Haimerich told me. I easily distinguished the Thuringians from the Saxons, and told them as I had been bid. They decided at once to surprise the Herzog in order to make him prisoner, and commanded me to show them the way. Now, I must tell you that there is a ravine in the slope of the Suona worn through the rock by water. It is so narrow that two men cannot pass it abreast, and so deep that the sun never reaches its bottom; the rocks towering high right and left. Up this path I led them, saying they could thus reach the top unseen by mortal eye. As they went up the defile, Haimerich, according to our arrangement, with some of his party, descended through the forest, and took his position behind them at the foot of the ravine. The first of them, meanwhile, having reached the top, I told them to go straight ahead, and they would soon come upon the Herzog. But, at this moment, our brave nobles were upon them, and their defeat was complete. Those which had not yet left the defile turned their backs and fled, pursued from the top, but there was no escape at the bottom. Haimerich and his followers received them man by man as they emerged from the ravine. Most were killed; some were taken prisoners. The Herzog had, by this time, been joined by the great body of his fighting men and, when he heard what Haimerich and a handful of Christian nobles had done, he was loud in their praise.

"One of the prisoners escaped. He fled into the Saxon camp to announce what had happened. They hastily rose to arms, but Hedan and his force were upon them, attacking them from different sides. It was a bloody encounter, but the Saxons were defeated. Hedan pursued them to where the Horsila joins the Wesra. There they gained their ships, and, moreover, the night closed in, else not a man would have escaped. The Herzog dispatched me to bring you the news of this great victory which the Lord hath given him, and he bids you to hold the men of God in loving care."

That was a sunbeam to Bellaheld's heart, while Geila saw but clouds on the horizon. Hedan's heathen enemies had been annihilated. He had been revenged on them by his Christian followers. It seemed nearly certain what his future course would be.

But the first thing which Bellaheld now did was to gather her Christian people about her to offer up thanks. There was no noise now to disturb their worship. When it was near dinner time, Geila sent two of her women, begging Bellaheld to join again the common meal in the hall, promising she should in no way be molested. Bellaheld hesitated a moment. Her Christian humility would have complied with Geila's request, but upon reflection, she saw that the latter would only presume upon her forbearance. She replied, therefore, that she would continue to take her meals in solitude. Then Geila grew alarmed and made a point of sending her the choicest morsels.

But the old Herzogin's wicked heart soon beat more lightly. Her maiden, Regiswind, had whispered to her important news—nothing less than that Gisilhar had been seen at Hochheim.

"Aha!" said Geila. "If Hedan cannot be brought to hate her for her religion's sake, he will do so for her infidelity. It is plain that there is some understanding between her and Gisilhar. What else should be the reason of his presence while my son is away? But we will watch them. I shall not prevent her meeting him in the cenoby. On the contrary—I shall be glad if I can prove it."

And behold, the very next morning, the maid Regiswind came to Bellaheld expressing an unexpected wish to join in the Christian worship. She was anxious, she said, about her soul, and desirous of knowing more of Bellaheld's God. The young Herzogin doubted her sincerity, but gave her leave. She chose the story of Ananias and Sapphira for the morning's portion, adding a few solemn words as to the power and holiness of God, before whom no falsehood could live. Regiswind trembled a little, but she continued to attend prayers.

Two or three days thus passed peacefully, but then came a night of grievous woe. Bellaheld was roused from sleep by the buffalo horn from the tower. She knew it meant alarm, and dressed in haste. A horseman arrived. Voices were loud in the courtyard, and, as she opened her shutter, a cry of horror passed from mouth to mouth. The "Herzog is dead—dead!" they cried, and Bellaheld sank in a swoon.

CHAPTER 8

TROUBLE AND ESCAPE

For, lo, they lie in wait for my soul: the mighty are gathered against me; not for my transgression, nor for my sin, O LORD. —Psalm 59:3

The Saxons collected their force on the other side of the Wesra, and, seemingly retiring along the bank of the river, they recrossed and doubled upon the enemy with the view of attacking him in the rear. Hedan, meanwhile, and his army, ferried over on rafts, but, finding the

Saxons had quitted the ground, he, too, returned to the right shore, intending to push northward the following day, when lo! he found himself overtaken by the foe, coming from a direction where he least expected them. The night had been chosen for the attack, and had it not been for Haimerich's vigilance, their success would have been instantaneous.

Faithful Haimerich, suspecting the sudden disappearance of the Saxons, would not leave the safety of the camp to the ordinary night watch, but posted himself with his bugle on an eminence beyond, keeping a careful lookout, aided by the growing moon. His ear caught the nearing sound of horses' hoofs, and presently his peering eye saw gleams of moonlight reflected on copper helmets. He gave the alarm which roused the camp. The Saxon vanguard was close in sight, but Haimerich kept his post, well knowing that the hill was too important a position to be lost. His incessant bugle call was the signal for urgent help. The Thuringians, understanding the import, hastened towards the hill. But the first of the Saxons were already upon him. Haimerich closed with three, who succumbed to his mighty strokes. But five more were ready to attack him. Jumping sideways, he succeeded in separating them, gaining the victory upon them also. He saw the Thuringians at the foot of the hill. If he could but hold out a few moments longer! The host of the enemy was upon him. Haimerich's sword, as a blade of lightning, flashed in all directions. He bled of twenty wounds, but his object was gained. He sank in death when the Thuringians came up behind him, and made good the position for which he gave his life.

The intention of the Saxons to force their adversary into the river was thereby frustrated. They now pushed upon the camp where Hedan, with a number of his nobles, received them. He succeeded in dividing them. One part was driven back on the hill, and finally dispersed. The others retreated more orderly, and, having crossed the Wesra by swimming, made preparation there for a final stand. Hedan ordered his troops to be ferried over, but this process was somewhat slow, as only a certain number at a time could thus get across. The Herzog was among the first, that he might dispose of each succeeding batch as they arrived.

The Saxons were ready for an attack sooner than he expected, and, pressing down upon the shore, they effectually hindered the further landing of the Thuringians. The Herzog, heading his little band, tried to oppose them, but the weight of the enemy drove back his followers upon the river. He found himself left alone with a few of his men, vainly trying to gain a retreat. Some Thuringian nobles, perceiving his strait from the other side of the Wesra, attempted to reach him by swimming, but they were still in the water when the wild shouts of the enemy announced that help came too late. Hedan had fallen, struck down by the blow of a club. The few men who had been able to stand by him to the last were disarmed and taken prisoners. The Thuringians saw how the victors stripped the Herzog of his helmet, shield, and sword, but lost sight of the body in the confusion which followed.

The right shore of the Wesra was in the hands of the Saxons. Nothing remained for the Thuringians on the other side but to retreat and gather their forces among the hills. Hedan's retainers, who had fallen into the hands of the enemy, were even now being butchered as a sacrifice to the war god, Eor.

Thus ran the woeful tale. Poor Bellaheld shut herself up in her chamber, weeping and trembling.

Geila had triumphed. Hard as a flint, she had listened to

the news of her son's death, but, turning to Bellaheld, she had exclaimed wrathfully, "This is the gods' revenge upon those who turned his heart from their service!"

Hedan had a cousin who owned a Burg in the Rhon. He was not a ruler to be desired, lacking even ordinary capabilities, but he was a heathen, and for Geila that was enough. "He must be chosen Herzog," said Geila to herself. That this would require some manipulation she knew, for the remaining nobles—most of whom were Christians, the heathen having fallen in the first encounter—would stand by Hedan's wife. It was necessary, therefore, to get rid of Bellaheld before they returned from the war.

And Geila had prepared her means. If Bellaheld was accused of infidelity to her husband, she must be brought to the fire ordeal, and, as no one could be judged innocent by that ordeal whose feet were not made of clay or stone, it would be easy to prove her guilt and ensure her death.

But the charge of infidelity could be easily founded upon the evidence that she had met with Gisilhar. And moreover, had she met with him lately in the cenoby, how should it be proved that such meetings had not taken place before? Geila and her priests had laid their plot, and while the faithful nobles were absent, there was none to prevent its being carried out.

On the following Sunday, Regiswind joined the number of those who accompanied Bellaheld to the oratory. And, so true seemed her attitude, that Bellaheld, having seen her tears, invited her after service to come with her to visit the Abbot. Little did she think who, in spite of all her prohibition, was again present in the cabin.

Geila anxiously awaited Regiswind's testimony. No sooner had she returned than she was required to give it.

"Gisilhar was with the Abbot," said the waiting maid, "but your suspicions are ill founded. No babe could be purer than our Herzogin. We had not entered the cabin when the Abbot met us, exclaiming, 'Retire, noble lady, unless you would meet him whose presence is hateful to you.' 'What!' she exclaimed, indignantly. 'Has he dared to show himself again, though you and I forbade him the cenoby?' 'He says,' replied the Abbot, 'that you are free of your oath now, the Herzog being dead, and that no law, either human or Divine, prevented your listening to his suit. He prays you to accept his protection in your present strait, and allow him to take you safely to the Herzog Theudo's land.'

" 'Tell him,' replied the Herzogin, 'that I charge him once more to leave Wirzburg, or I myself will ask my mother-in-law to consider him a prisoner. If he is here on his master's business, he should have brought his credentials to the Wirtsburg instead of hiding himself as a wrong-doer.' 'I cannot blame you,' said the Abbot, 'yet you speak in anger, noble lady. You forget the dangers awaiting you on the Burg and should not spurn lightly a protector like Gisilhar.'

" 'I need no protection save God's,' returned she. 'What right, indeed, has this Gisilhar to count upon my accepting his unwelcome suit? I have seen him but twice in my life; once in the presence of the Herzog, my husband, and once when he took me to my mother's dying bed. I own I did not dislike him that first time of our meeting, and, if the Herzog had not come between, who knows but what I might have listened to him, but now I thank God who led me otherwise, for now I see he is but a man who is guided by his own selfish will rather than by Christian duty. He knows what I have suffered innocently on his account, and yet he expects me to follow his desires no sooner than my husband is dead, lending colour thereby to the very suspicion which persecuted me and shamed my Christian calling! I say, no! And I repeat, unless he leaves the land immediately, I myself will apprise my enemies of his presence.' Thus spoke the Herzogin, and, leaving the Abbot, she returned with me to the Burg."

"Were any of her women present at this conversation?" demanded Geila.

"None but myself," said Regiswind.

"That is lucky," rejoined Geila. "Thou wilt swear to the priests that thou overheardst her secret whispering with Gisilhar, and that she has agreed to his carrying her off to Theudo's land."

"I will never give such testimony!" exclaimed Regiswind, indignantly. "What! Should I betray the innocent Herzogin? That may be work for a heathen, but not for a Christian woman, as I am now."

"Thou, a Christian?" cried Geila, clutching her by the arm. "A pretty story indeed!"

"I am," repeated Regiswind solemnly. "You have commanded me yourself to join the worship of God. You have brought me within reach of the fire which has quickened my conscience and brought light to my darkened soul. It is a fearful thing to fall into the hands of the living God, but it is blessed to become His child and taste His love. Oh, if you could have heard the Herzogin pray for her husband, recommending him to the mercy of his Redeemer. And if you could hear her intercede for you, that you might receive grace and forgiveness of sin."

"Sin! Dares she charge me with sin, the impudent beggar? And thou, graceless minion, darest thou repeat it to my face?" screamed Geila, beside herself with rage, and ill-treating the poor girl till the blood streamed from her nose and mouth. "I'll teach thee to know thy betters and obey my will."

"You may beat me; kill me if it be your will. I can die for the truth and for our dear Lady Bellaheld!" replied the brave girl, and swooned away under Geila's cruel hand.

Geila, having spent her fury, stopped to consider. What if the waiting woman, who evidently had become a Christian, should betray her intentions, proving them by the very lie which Geila had just attempted to put into her mouth! That must not be. Regiswind must be silenced.

The old Herzogin, having sent for two of her priests, informed them that the girl had forsworn the gods, and should, therefore, be made one of the victims at the great sacrifice she intended to offer up to Woden in memory of her son's death. And poor Regiswind, waking from her swoon, found herself a helpless prisoner in a hole underground. She knew the place, and that it was used for those only who were destined to be slaughtered in honor of the gods. She knew her fate, but was willing to yield her life, accepting a baptism of blood for the baptism of water that should seal her covenant.

Bellaheld missed her at prayers the following morning, but none of her women knew anything about her. "Had Geila sent her away? Or had she fled to the cenoby, fearing Geila's anger? Or again, was her conversion mere pretence?" thought Bellaheld, not knowing what to make of her absence.

But explanation was given by Geila herself, who entered Bellaheld's chamber on Tuesday, saying, "To-morrow we yield sacrifice to Woden on account of my son's death. Regiswind is one of the appointed victims. We shall expect thy presence. Thou shalt join the procession; the path must be strewn with raven's feathers and mistletoe by thy hands."

"I shall not join the wicked show," said Bellaheld, starting in just anger, "and no harm shall be done to Regiswind!"

"Not without thy permission, perhaps?" sneered Geila. "No one has asked thee for it. Thou wilt do as thou art bid."

"You forget," said Bellaheld, "that you will have to give an account to the nobles when they return from the war."

"They are far distant now, and who knows how many of them will return? The Saxons advance victoriously. Meanwhile, it is thy business to yield obedience. I am mistress here, as thou seest." She turned and left her.

Bellaheld fell to her knees and called to God for help. She resolved to retire at once to the cenoby for protection, but, going to the door, she found it barred and locked, two of Geila's men keeping watch below.

Again she fell to her knees, earnestly praying for strength to bear and strength to withstand; for peace in sorrow and submission to whatever her God would have her bear. She considered the past, and felt comfort in the thought that she had not listened to Gisilhar's suit. "It is blessed," she said, "to suffer innocently."

Night came, but she was left in darkness. She lay down on her couch dressed as she was, and so peaceful was her heart in answer to her prayer that she slept like a child. She woke, hearing a gentle knocking, which seemed to come from the garret room beyond. Reflecting that no one could have entered that room save through her own chamber, she thought she must have been dreaming. But the knocking was repeated and a deep voice whispered presently, "Open the door, noble lady! It is I, Pillung. I cannot find the latch."

She undid the bolt and stepped aside, waiting for an explanation. She could not see him enter, for there was no ray of light. She scarcely heard his cautious advance, but again he whispered, "Flee, noble lady! The way is prepared. I have loosened some planks in the outer wall. Flee, flee at once!

Regiswind is imprisoned to be slaughtered to-morrow. I, too, am a chosen victim, and a more terrible fate awaits yourself."

"Where are my women?" asked the Herzogin.

"They have escaped, and await you anxiously by the river."

"And where is Gisilhar?"

"Alas, that he had not left!" said Pillung dolefully. "His would be a strong arm in your defense! But he disappeared on Sunday, none could tell whither."

"The Lord be praised!" whispered Bellaheld.

"Do not tarry!" urged the faithful Pillung, and he led her to the passage he had made, where a rope ladder hung suspended. They reached the inner court, which was guarded at night, but it so happened that the man on duty was a former companion of Pillung, and good-natured enough to listen to his pleading. Before attempting Bellaheld's escape, he had told him of the miserable fate awaiting her, and he, remembering her many deeds of kindness, promised not to stand in her way. Pillung still feared treachery, but the man was true to his word, and the fugitives got safely away.

They went straight to the river. Bellaheld, on no account, would allow the men of God to be privy to her flight, thereby endangering their own safety, but, having joined her women, she at once took boat, Pillung being of the party. Not a word was spoken. The little craft was borne away by the current and presently, when the women plied the oars while Pillung steered, the boat shot swiftly along and passed Hochheim, the inhabitants of which slept their unsuspecting sleep.

Not till the forenoon was Bellaheld missed from her chamber. Geila first of all had the cenoby searched, although she could hardly expect Bellaheld to be hiding so dangerously near. Not finding her there, the heathen servants were dispatched to scour the neighborhood, but chiefly the roads leading to Bavaria. They returned without her, and Geila was delighted. It was just what she wanted. For this very reason had she, in Pillung's hearing, given vent to those threats which he repeated to Bellaheld, and which she meant to be acted upon by their flight. And now the young Herzogin had actually fled by stealth—for what reason was known to Geila only.

CHAPTER 9

PEACE AT LAST

I shall give thee the heathen for thine inheritance. —Psalm 2:8

On the evening preceding the night on which Bellaheld received the news of her husband's death, two men of God were wending their way through a forest in Hessian land. The long robe of undyed sheep's wool was held up by the girdle, their heads were covered with the broad-brimmed hat, the pilgrim's staff was in their hand, and they strode away actively, bent on reaching their journey's end before the night. One of them, tall and thoughtful, had reached the riper years of manhood, his younger fair-haired companion being scarcely more than five and twenty.

"Look yonder, Adelhelm," said the former. "We now see the wooded heights of Thuringia rising in the purple sunset. The Wesra cannot be far. I think we near the frontier. Alas, I tremble for Brother Lando! If it be true that the Saxons have crossed the Wesra, pillaging the land as far as the Hessian frontier, he may have fared grievously in his lonely cell!"

"I, too, am full of fears," replied the younger, "for, though his cell lies apart in a forest glen, it is not far distant from the Wesra."

"I trust," rejoined the elder, "that he may have evaded the danger, and found shelter with one of those Hessian nobles who have accepted his preaching."

"I doubt not, brother, but that his spiritual children would protect him in trouble."

The former assented, but continued, after a while, "Yet I hope that thou art not without the box of healing ointment, lest we should find him in trouble and wounded perchance."

"I have it with me, brother, and whatever may be needed besides. But see, we are at the mouth of the glen, and yonder is Lando's cabin. It seems safe, and the little garden undisturbed."

"Yet there is no sign of our brother," interposed the elder traveler anxiously. "God grant that we may find him safe!"

The two men quickened their steps. Two lambs were grazing happily on a meadow, and a fallow deer, which Lando had tamed, looked at them with quiet eyes. They opened the door of the cabin and found Brother Lando on a low stool before his bed, bending toward the couch, and so engrossed that he heard them not. There was not sufficient light in the cabin for them to distinguish the object of his care, but when Adelhelm closed the door with a creak, Lando started anxiously.

"Peace be with thee!" said the elder. "We have come, brother, trusting to find thee safe."

"God be thanked!" cried Lando. "It is Willebrord's voice. And who is thy companion?"

"Brother Adelhelm is with me, who joined me at Erfurt."

"Blessed be your coming in!" said Lando. "But let me strike a light that I may see your face."

The pale glimmer of the lamp soon lit up the humble space. The travelers saw that the venerable Lando stood before them safe and sound, but they also saw the figure of a dead man on the couch. The lower part of the corpse was covered with the bear skin, but the upper part lay bare. On the chest, a shining carbuncle[31] hung suspended on a golden chain. The head was bound up with a cloth.

"How comest thou by this dead man in thy cabin?" asked Willebrord.

"He seems dead, yet there are no signs of death," said Lando. "He has lain here three days already. There is neither breath nor pulse, yet it is not the pallor of death, and he is scarcely cold."

"Didst thou bring him from the battlefield?" asked Adelhelm.

"I did, brother. When the uproar had ceased, I ventured forth in the shelter of the night. I found that there had been a deadly encounter; that the wild Saxons had been on our side of the river, but that they had left again, and that the Thuringians also had disappeared from their place of encampment. Then I bethought me whether some poor wounded warrior might not require help, and looking about, I came upon the ashes of what evidently had been a great funeral pyre, leaving no doubt that the conquerors had butchered their prisoners and burnt them as a sacrifice to Eor. The corpses of those which had fallen in the encounter were lying about, already a prey to the crows and ravens which haunt the battlefield. I turned to quit the ghastly scene when I perceived a crow settling in a body, and leave it again almost immediately. I went nearer and saw it was a fine manly figure in buffalo armor, but without sword or helmet, lying pale and still. I touched his hand, and it was warm. I lifted him on my shoulders and brought him to my cabin, and here he has been lying these three days—pale, motionless, without breath or sign of life, but warm. I have found no wound on him but the marks of a blow on his head, which I keep, therefore, bandaged with cold water. I was trying to listen to the beat of his heart when you entered. I had vainly done so before, but this time it seemed as though there were a slight pulsation."

"Let us try," said Adelhelm, plucking a small feather from a tame pigeon which shared Lando's cabin and placing the fluffy down upon the lips of the lifeless warrior, where the feather trembled almost imperceptibly at measured intervals. "He lives; he breathes. The Lord be praised!" cried Adelhelm.

"Let us call upon our God," said Willebrord, kneeling, "that He may be gracious unto him and restore his life."

Willebrord would not leave Lando's cabin before they knew the Lord's will concerning the unknown warrior, and whether he would die or live. They hoped for the latter.

Adelhelm went to prepare a couch for himself and Brother Willebrord, while Lando busied himself in getting ready a humble supper for his guests. Willebrord, in the meantime, watched the pale-faced man, again and again listening for the beating of his heart. And it did beat more and more frequently. They took their supper in quiet haste and, returning to the bedside, wetted the sick man's lips, which seemed less white than before, and behold, he swallowed the water thirstily. They repeated the attempt. The breathing became more and more regular. Towards midnight, he opened his eyes, and, seeing men about him with unknown faces, though otherwise of a well-known dress and appearance, he closed them again with a sigh, and sighing again, he whispered, "Bellaheld!"

"We shall leave him, body and soul, to the care of the men of God, returning ourselves to the Wirtsburg."

It was on a Wednesday morning that Bellaheld's flight had been discovered. That also was the day sacred to Woden, when the great sacrifice in memory of Hedan's death was to be celebrated, and Regiswind should be killed by Woden's priest. But Geila was obliged to postpone her intentions. Bellaheld's escape required half the inhabitants of the Burg to be dispatched on the search, and the proposed sacrifice must be honored by the presence of all. Moreover, Regiswind had been greatly disfigured by Geila's blows; her face was covered with unsightly marks of violence, which would not heal in the damp hole assigned to her abode, yet she must present a fair countenance to be offered up to the god, for which reason a respite was granted until the Wednesday a fortnight hence.

The evil day came round. Not in the forest, as was usual, but in the inner court the pyre was raised. Triumphant Geila had chosen the very place where her husband, Gozbert, had renounced all heathen worship. The whole household was gathered in a circle, and, as the ill-fated horses and boars were being prepared for the knife, wild songs to Woden rose on the air. The tumult was heard as far as the cenoby, filling the congregation with grief and horror.

The chief victim was now called for, and Regiswind was dragged to the spot. One of the priests held the knife, while another bared her bosom to receive it. She prayed aloud to God in heaven. Her words were overpowered by the bloodthirsty howling of her murderers, but louder than this, even, resounded a piercing cry of horror, and Geila fell to the ground.

The silence which followed was more terrible even than the noise. What was it? The eyes of all were upon Geila. But she, writhing on the ground, pointed in agony to the Burg gate.

"What evil work is being done here?" cried Hedan imperiously, for it was he who had appeared at the entrance, followed by a number of his Christian nobles. None dared answer. Regiswind only, after a while, found strength to give a trembling account of what had happened and what was being done.

"And where is Bellaheld?" demanded the Herzog.

"Hiding, no doubt, in her chamber," said Regiswind, who knew nothing of her flight. "They drove her from her rightful place in the hall long ago."

But now Geila jumped up, rejoicing in the news she thought she could give, and cried with evil laughter, "She has fled from the Burg, ashamed to stay. It is a fortnight since she disappeared in the dead of the night!"

"God forbid!" exclaimed the Herzog. "A great length indeed thou must have driven her, before she could take such a step. Give me back my wife!"

"Ask Gisilhar to give her back to thee!" sneered Geila. "I am innocent of her flight. Gisilhar has been seen in the cenoby. I doubt me not but he knows where she may be hiding."

"He is here, and ready to answer your charge against the noble Herzogin!" Gisilhar himself stepped forth from among the warriors.

"I was in the cenoby, as you say, and I had ample proof of your cruelty to the God-fearing lady. I did offer to save her from her heathen surroundings, forgetting, in my selfish blindness, that it was the Lord who had placed her there. But she steadfastly refused to accept my protection to Reginsburg, and even refused to see me; yes, more than this, she commanded me to leave Wirzburg unless I would have her acquaint you herself of my presence. Seeing she was in earnest, but knowing her danger, and still desirous of saving her, I rode off at once to call together the Christian nobles who, I knew, would gather round their Herzogin. But it cost me days and nights before I found our brave Thuringians. They had beaten the Saxons, making good the defeat sustained by the Wesra, and were even then pursuing them beyond the frontier of their own country. And when, at last, I came upon them as they returned victoriously, we fell in with a Hessian freeman who spoke to us, saying, 'If ye be Thuringians, sirs, and anxious perchance to see your own Herzog again, follow me, for your Herzog is not dead, as ye deem, but living with Lando and Willebrord, the men of God.' And he showed us the way to the Crossburg beyond the Wesra, where we found the noble Hedan healed in body and soul, and we witnessed his baptism by Father Willebrord."

"I can add to this testimony," now said Regiswind, addressing herself to Geila, "and indeed I have nothing to say to the noble Gisilhar. You expected me to bear false testimony against her, and when I refused, you ill-treated me with you own hands and condemned me to a cruel death."

"All of this will not explain her flight," said Hedan, turning again to his mother. "Once more I ask thee to what length thou hast driven her, before she could leave the Burg?"

"I can tell it, so please you," now spoke the doorkeeper who was on guard that night. "She threatened Pillung to sacrifice him together with Regiswind, and she threatened the Herzogin to hold her a prisoner and bring her to the fire ordeal. But me she commanded not to hinder the lady's flight, if she chose to go."

"Whither is she gone? Give me back my wife!" cried Hedan, beside himself with pity and grief, taking hold of his mother by the arm, yet dropping it again immediately.

"She is my mother," added he, "I will not be her judge nor her keeper. I give her to your care, my nobles. Hold her safe, lest she work further sorrow."

One of the nobles, Ruodbert by name, accepted the charge, and led her away with him to his Burg. The heathen priests were tied and imprisoned by Hedan's command.

"Woe is me to be bereaved of so faithful a wife!" said he, "yet it is God's just retribution for my sinful distrust of her. I am not worthy of such a wife. I pray God to make me better than I was. I would fain ride in search of her, not stopping day or night, that I might find her again, yet the ruler is tied to his Wirtsburg by all-important duties. But thou, Brother Gisilhar, thou mayest go in search of her, and perchance bring her back to me."

Gisilhar, accepting the trust, rode off at once, directing his horse's head to Hochheim, hoping to learn of Totman whether Bellaheld had any relatives to whom she might have gone in her distress. But the venerable Totman had departed this life. Gertrude had some recollection of having heard Mechild mention an uncle of Bellaheld's, but where he lived she knew not, nor could she remember his name.

Autumn and winter passed, and Hedan had no news of Bellaheld. All his attempts to hear of her proved fruitless.

Gisilhar, too, had returned from an unsuccessful search, and was again at Herzog Theudo's court. Spring had come to the country, when one day a messenger arrived at Reginsburg, sent by the Frankish king, Childebert. Speaking to Theudo and his nobles, he related much of new cenobies he had seen on his journey, and how the Gospel was finding entrance everywhere. Amongst other places, this messenger had visited a school at Moguntia, founded by a niece of Abbot-Bishop Sigfrid for the Christian training of young maidens. Sigfrid's niece herself was but young, he said, and had fled with her women and a maimed man-servant from a heathen mother-in-law.

Gisilhar started. "When was this?" he exclaimed.

"Some months ago," replied the messenger. "The young lady had bought the land for her foundation, paying for it with twelve silver shields and twelve black steeds, which her uncle gave her as her share of the property come to her by her Irish parentage."

"Yes! Yes!" cried Gisilhar, "and her name is Bellaheld!"

"It may be," said the Frank. "I do not remember her name."

Within two days of this conversation, Herzog Hedan received a letter by Gisilhar's fleetest runner. Hedan tore it open and turned pale, then red. He gave immediate orders for a vessel to be got ready, and, having put the Burg in charge of a trusted freeman, he took boat, accompanied by a suitable retinue, and sailed down the Main. Regiswind was of the party.

It was a pleasant journey between the wooded heights, but Hedan's heart grew heavier day by day. It was early in

April, just about a year since he first met Bellaheld among the beech trees. Sadness filled his soul as he thought of that meeting. "Will she come to me now, if I find her again?" said he within himself. "She cannot but have heard by this time that I am alive. Why has she not returned to me? Or is it all a mistake, and the young lady is not my Bellaheld?"

On the sixth day, at noon, the vessel was carried by the Main into the stately Rhine and anchored before Moguntia. Pillung was tending the cattle on a meadow, when, lifting his eyes, he beheld a young woman walking swiftly along. But, seeing him, she turned and came up to him. He seemed to know her, yet waited doubtfully another moment.

"Regiswind, is it thyself, or a spirit?" he said.

"It is myself, Pillung," she said smiling. "Why shouldest thou take me for a ghost?"

"But thou wast going to be—" and he was unable to continue.

"Going to be sacrificed to Woden," said she, taking up his sentence. "Yes, but by the grace of God I have escaped. I found shelter with an honest man, and am now in the service of one who has shipping on the Main."

"The Lord be praised who saved thee!" rejoined Pillung. "But tell me, is it true that our Herzog lives? We heard some time ago that peace was restored to the Wirtsburg, and that a ruler had returned. We thought that perchance one of Herzog Hedan's relatives might have been chosen by the people, but quite lately we learned that our own Herzog Hedan had come back from the war. We could not believe it. Our much-honored lady cried sore at the news. 'Is he indeed alive, and has he not made search for me? He could but have inquired of Totman, who would surely have told him that my uncle is Abbot-Bishop of Moguntia. But, I fear me, my husband is offended that I left the Burg. His mother, Geila, has turned his heart from me, and I dare not venture back to the Wirtsburg.' So she says, and tears are her portion every day. But now thou art come with certain news of the Herzog. Tell me, how is he minded?"

"How should I know?" replied Regiswind, keeping up her role. "Did I not tell thee I escaped to an honest man? In those days none knew what had become of the Herzog."

"True," assented Pillung. "But now hasten to the Herzogin. She will receive thee gladly. Would I could leave the herd to go with thee."

"I am on my way to her, but not alone," said Regiswind. "My master, who brought me hither on his ship, desires to consult her concerning a maiden to be educated. Dost thou think she will receive him? He is awaiting my answer, and wishes me to take him to Bellaheld, for I told him I was in her service formerly."

"The Herzogin receives anyone that requires to see her," said Pillung. "Go, fetch thy master and go with him."

"He follows me yonder. Farewell till we meet again." And Pillung watched her speed away towards a man who, from his dress and bearing, seemed a shipmaster, as she had described him. But Pillung could not see his face light up with joy at the account Regiswind gave him. He watched them walk away towards Bellaheld's present home. The "shipmaster" was sufficiently disguised by a wig and a false beard, appearing an elderly man in his adopted garb. They entered the courtyard leading to the school, and, having inquired for the Lady Bellaheld, were directed to an antechamber leading to the hall in which Bellaheld taught her youthful charges. Regiswind remained outside while her master entered the anteroom. With beating heart, he saw the door open which led from the hall, and Bellaheld, in a simple woolen robe, stepped forth. A sleeping babe lay on her arm.

"What is your desire?" she asked kindly.

"I would speak to you, noble Herzogin," replied he, with an unusually deep voice.

"Not Herzogin, but humble teacher," she corrected him quickly, almost sharply.

"Excuse me," continued the visitor, "but I was wont to call you thus in former days, when you used to join in worship at the Wirzburg cenoby."

"Alas!" she cried. "What times are these you bring to my mind!"

"Yes," said he, "in those days your husband lived and had you by his side. But you were not happy."

"Who are you," interrupted Bellaheld sternly, "to speak to me thus? Those who do their duty are ever happy."

"Yes, yes," assented he, "you did your duty, but he treated you unworthily."

"How dare you accuse my husband to my face? If this is all your business with me, I have no more to say to you." And she turned to go.

"Stay, noble lady, and let me deliver my commission." He touched her arm, and the little boy awoke, crowing lustily. But he, taking from his bosom a carbuncle suspended by a golden chain, hung it round the child's neck.

"What is this?" cried Bellaheld. "How do you come by this jewel, the Herzog's heirloom, which his own father put on him when he was yet a babe in arms, and which he never parted with, to my knowledge!"

"True," said he, "the Herzog's heirloom has always passed to the son and heir with the father's first blessing."

"But how do you come by it? Have they robbed my husband in death and sold you the jewel? Oh, say what you would have, and let me redeem it!"

"I cannot sell it! It belongs to the child now to whom it passed from my hand. But no enemy stole this jewel, and the Herzog never parted with it. Have you never heard the report, lady, that Hedan is not dead, but lives?"

"I have heard it," she said with uncertain, almost frightened voice, "but it seemed more than I could believe."

"Why so? There are others who live, though you believed them dead—Regiswind, for instance."

And Regiswind entered. Bellaheld, seeing her, gave a cry, and, putting down the child, she clasped the waiting-woman in her arms. She could not speak.

"Yes, dear Herzogin," said Regiswind, taking up the child and fondling it, "I am indeed returned from the very gates of death. The knife was lifted to slay me when the Herzog appeared whom we had mourned as dead. And the Lord has brought him to life in a double sense—he is a Christian now, and a true believer. And what would you say, dear lady, if he himself were present to confirm this happy news?"

Bellaheld turned uneasily. The "shipmaster" had thrown off his disguise, and now, with a cry of joy, she was clasped to her husband's heart.

Three days later, they set out to return to the Wirtsburg, where they arrived towards the end of April, the school of Moguntia having passed to the care of another teacher.

Joyously rose the hymns of praise and thanksgiving from both cenobies when the ship, drawn up the river by six stout horses, returned with the happy pair. No sooner had they entered their own Wirtsburg than a servant announced a man of God coming from Hessian land with a special message to the Herzog. He had arrived the day before, and was waiting in the cenoby.

"That is Willebrord," exclaimed Hedan. "Bring him hither speedily. He is a welcome guest and shall bless our happy union."

It was Willebrord indeed, bringing news which moved both Hedan and Bellaheld greatly. "I have visited Ruodbert on my journey hither," said he, "and have seen your mother, Anna."

"Her name is Geila," interrupted Hedan.

"It was Geila," said the man of God. "She is Anna now. I learnt from Ruodbert that she has been ailing through the winter. She had times of great despondency, but repulsed every attempt to approach her with spiritual help. I went in to her. 'What is thy desire, thou man of God?' cried she. 'Hast thou come to call me to judgment? Thy God is terrible, powerful, victorious, and no lie can live when He speaketh.'

" 'Yes, Geila,' I said, 'He is the Holy and Just Who hath sent me. He has seen thy heart, that it is black, and thy sins, that they are as scarlet. He passed by thee, and saw thee polluted in thine own blood, and said unto thee, "Live." Yea, thou shalt live through the blood of His only Son, shed for thee on the cross. He, the merciful Redeemer, will heal thee, Geila; He will snatch thee from death and darkness. He will take thee by the hand and bring thee to His Father, saying, "Father, forgive her. I have borne her iniquities." And, behold, she seized my hand with a torrent of tears, continuing in anguish for hours. But on the seventh day she received baptism. Her health is broken. She has not many days to live, and is anxious to see you and the Herzogin that she may not die without your forgiveness."

Hedan and Bellaheld set off at once for Ruodbert's Burg,

to behold there the greatest triumph of Gospel grace, and to assure the dying mother of their forgiving love.

Having returned to the Wirtsburg after her death, Hedan felt desirous of proving his gratitude to Willebrord, his spiritual father, and did so by a grant of land, enabling him thereby to found new cenobies in the northern part of Thuringia, which was still a stronghold of heathenism. The deed of gift, dated April 30th, 704, is still extant, by which the Herzog made over to "Willebrord, his father in Christ," his possessions at Arnstadt and Weimar. Willebrord charged his disciple, Adelhelm, with the founding of these new cenobies.

In the summer, Hedan gave Regiswind to his servant Pillung to wife, thereby meeting the desire of both their hearts. The wedding was on a Friday, according to ancient usage, which appropriated this day for serving folk. Freemen and lords always married on a Tuesday.

The Christian congregation spread and grew, and, as the old cenoby could no longer hold the numbers, Hedan built a large, beautiful church at the foot of his Wirtsburg.

And God blessed Princess Bellaheld and her husband with another child besides their little son, Thuring, giving them a daughter, whom they called Immina. The boy Thuring was a delicate child, and died before his father. Thus the rulership passed to another house. Immina lived to see the Irish cenobies brought to the pope's subjection, having first been forced to yield to the Frankish supremacy by Pepin d'Heristal.

Centuries of darkness came upon the Church but, though hiding the pure light of the Gospel, they could not quench it. The Lord had prepared another time when, in Thuringia and elsewhere, men of God arose, strong to wield the sword of the Spirit and tear asunder the lying tissue of human intervention, preaching the old unchangeable Gospel truth of Christ, the only Savior of men.

GLOSSARY OF TERMS

1. Herzog - A lord and leader, literally, with the ancient Germans; one who went before them in battle; "duke" being the modern equivalent.

2. Oratory - A place allotted for prayer; a place for public worship.

3. Castle of the Wirt - That is, master of the house and lord of the land. From it is derived Wirtsburg, changed to Wurzburg, the town of our days, on the Main. In the course of this story Wirtsburg will denote the Herzog's residence on the hill; Wirzburg being the distinctive appellation for the missionary settlement at its foot.

4. Cenoby - A place where persons live in community.

5. Erin - An ancient name of Ireland.

6. Moguntia - Present-day Mainz

7. Refectory - A room of refreshment; properly, a hall or apartment in convents and monasteries, where a moderate repast is taken.

8. Nunc Dimittis - Simeon's prayer in Luke 2:29-32, often used as a liturgical song.

9. Cupola - In architecture, a spherical vault on the top of an edifice; a dome, or the round top of a dome.

10. Nave - The middle or body of a church extending from the balluster or rail of the door, to the chief choir.

11. Belfry - That part of a steeple, or other building, in which a bell is hung.

12. Apoplexy - A sudden deprivation of all sense and voluntary motion, occasioned by repletion or whatever interrupts the action of the nerves upon the muscles.

13. Greaves - Armor for the legs; a sort of boots.

14. Reginsburg - Modern Regensburg - Ratisbon

15. Retainer - One who is kept in service; an attendant; as the retainers of the ancient princes and nobility.

16. Transalpine - Lying or being beyond the Alps in regard to Rome, that is, on the north or west of the Alps; as Transalpine Gaul.

17. Interdicted - Forbidden; prohibited.

18. Walhalla - Also Valhalla: In Norse mythology, the hall of Odin where slain warriors are received.

19. Hel - Hades

20. Aurochs - A species of ox, whose bones are found in gravel and alluvial soil.

21. Matins - Morning worship or service; morning prayers or songs.

22. Valkyr - In Norse mythology, a maiden of Odin who conducts slain warriors to Walhalla.

23. Sumpter - A horse that carries clothes or furniture; a baggage-horse; usually called a pack-horse.

24. Chattels - Items of personal property.

25. Folkthing - Assembly of the people. Parliament in Denmark and Sweden is still called "Folkthing."

26. Caitiff - One who is base, despicable, or cowardly.

27. Palfrey - A small horse fit for ladies.

28. Lutetia - Present-day Paris

29. Pellucid feldspar - A type of crystalline rock which admits maximum passage of light without distortion or diffusion.

30. Jerkin - A jacket; a short coat; a close waistcoat.

31. Carbuncle - Any of several red stones, most particularly the garnet.

THE IRISH COMMUNION HYMN

Translated on pages 23-24, is given as follows in Dr. Todd's
Book of Hymns of the Ancient Church of Ireland

Sancti venite,
Christi corpus sumite
Sanctum bibentes,
Quo redempti sanguinem.

Salvati Christi
Corpore et sanguine,
A quo refecti
Laudes dicamus Deo.

Dator salutis
Christus filius Dei
Mundum salvarit
Per crucem et sanguinem.

Pro universis
Immolatus Dominus
Ipse Sacerdos
Existit et Hostia

Lege preceptum
Immolari hostias
Qua adumbrantur
Divina mysteria.

Lucis indultor
Et Salvator omnium
Praeclaram sanctis
Largitur est gratiam.

Accedant omnes
Pura mentes creduli
Suman aeternam
Salutis custodiam.

Sanctorum custos
Rector quoque Dominus
Vitae perennis
Largitur credentibus.

Coelestem panem
Dat esurientibus
De fonte vivo
Praebet sitientibus.

Alpha et Omega
Ipse Christus Dominus
Venit, venturus
Judicare homines.

PASS ON THE FAITH WITH
Timeless Christian Classics
from Generations

Christian Literature Restored for a New Generation

Check out the Timeless Christian Classics at:
Generations.org

CHRISTIAN DISCIPLESHIP CURRICULUM